When He Turned In Her Direction, Time Stopped, The Earth Freezing On Its Axis.

Their gazes met and held, like magnets to metal.

Neither blinked. Neither broke the bond. They stared at each other from across the room.

Emily's mouth went dry. Within an instant, he'd left her breathless. He wasn't flirting. It was more than that. Much more. He watched her with masculine recognition, as if he knew what it was like to touch her, to hold her, to run his hands over every inch of her body.

Dear Reader,

Welcome to Silhouette Desire and another month of sensual tales. Our compelling continuity DYNASTIES: THE DANFORTHS continues with the story of a lovely Danforth daughter whose well-being is threatened and the hot U.S. Navy SEAL assigned to protect her. Maureen Child's *Man Beneath the Uniform* gives new meaning to the term *sleepover!*

Other series this month include TEXAS CATTLEMAN'S CLUB: THE STOLEN BABY with Cindy Gerard's fabulous *Breathless for the Bachelor*. Seems this member of the Lone Star state's most exclusive club has it bad for his best friend's sister. Lucky lady! And Rochelle Alers launches a brand-new series, THE BLACKSTONES OF VIRGINIA, with *The Long Hot Summer,* which is set amid the fascinating world of horse-breeding.

Anne Marie Winston singes the pages with her steamy almost-marriage-of-convenience story, *The Marriage Ultimatum*. And in *Cherokee Stranger* by Sheri WhiteFeather, a man gets a second chance with a woman who wants him for her first time. Finally, welcome brand-new author Michelle Celmer with *Playing by the Baby Rules,* the story of a woman desperate for a baby and the hunky man who steps up to give her exactly what she wants.

Here's hoping Silhouette Desire delivers exactly what *you* desire in a powerful, passionate and provocative read!

Best,

Melissa Jeglinski

Melissa Jeglinski
Senior Editor, Silhouette Desire

Please address questions and book requests to:
Silhouette Reader Service
U.S.: 3010 Walden Ave., P.O. Box 1325, Buffalo, NY 14269
Canadian: P.O. Box 609, Fort Erie, Ont. L2A 5X3

CHEROKEE STRANGER

SHERI WHITEFEATHER

Silhouette® Desire

Published by Silhouette Books

America's Publisher of Contemporary Romance

SILHOUETTE BOOKS

ISBN 0-373-76563-0

CHEROKEE STRANGER

Printed in U.S.A.

Books by Sheri WhiteFeather

Silhouette Desire

Warrior's Baby #1248
Skyler Hawk: Lone Brave #1272
Jesse Hawk: Brave Father #1278
Cheyenne Dad #1300
Night Wind's Woman #1332
Tycoon Warrior #1364
Cherokee #1376
Comanche Vow #1388
Cherokee Marriage Dare #1478
Sleeping with Her Rival #1496
Cherokee Baby #1509
Cherokee Dad #1523
The Heart of a Stranger #1527
Cherokee Stranger #1563

SHERI WHITEFEATHER

lives in Southern California and enjoys ethnic dining, attending powwows and visiting art galleries and vintage clothing stores near the beach. Since her one true passion is writing, she is thrilled to be a part of the Silhouette Desire line. When she isn't writing, she often reads until the wee hours of the morning.

Sheri's husband, a member of the Muscogee Creek Nation, inspires many of her stories. They have a son, a daughter and a trio of cats—domestic and wild. She loves to hear from her readers. You may write to her at: P.O. Box 17146, Anaheim Hills, California 92817. Visit her Web site at www.SheriWhiteFeather.com.

DEDICATION

First of all, I would like to thank the Silhouette copy editors, who never fail to accommodate my lengthy dedications. This story involved extensive research on skin cancer and I greatly appreciate the doctors, nurses and hospital librarians who provided information. If I made any technical errors, I apologize. The stages and treatment of melanoma vary from patient to patient. I would also like to thank my mother, Lee Bundy, who helped me research this book. She is a remarkable lady and breast cancer survivor. Tara Gavin at Silhouette is receiving heartfelt thanks for her suggestions and input regarding this story. Another acknowledgment goes out to avid Silhouette reader Elizabeth Benway, for her stirring Web site tribute to her sister, Beth, a young mother and breast cancer survivor. To Lyndee Lightfoot, the project coordinator at the Lewiston Chamber of Commerce, for providing information about Lewiston, Idaho, and the surrounding areas. To the United States government for WITSEC, the Witness Security Program, which inspired the premise of this story. If I made any errors, please forgive me. I researched WITSEC to the best of my ability.

One

As the mellow tune echoed through the jukebox's hollow speakers, the tall, dark stranger made another selection.

Emily Chapman scooted to the edge of her seat. Everything about the stranger fascinated her, even his taste in music. So far, he'd chosen love songs, tragic ballads steeped in emotion, lyrics that defied his hard-edged stance.

He turned away from the jukebox, and she watched him through curious eyes.

Was he a ball-busting country boy or a street-smart city dweller? She couldn't quite tell. Either way, he carried himself with a wary, don't-mess-with-me gait.

He wore jeans, a white T-shirt and a denim jacket. His medium-length hair fell across his forehead in a rebellious black line, nearly shielding his eyes. His face, shadowed by the dim light, proved strong and angular.

Ignoring the other patrons, the small scatter of people in the bar, he proceeded to his table, where he'd left a bottle of domestic beer. Next he slouched in his seat, kicked his booted feet onto the rail of an empty chair and lifted his drink, taking a long, hard swallow.

"Here you go." The waitress brought Emily's wine, blocking her view, shutting out the intriguing stranger.

Caught off guard, she shifted her attention to the other woman, a middle-aged, kiss-my-grits redhead whose nametag identified her as Meg. "Thank you."

"You're welcome, hon." Meg motioned to the door that led to the kitchen. "But your appetizer isn't ready yet. It'll be a few more minutes."

"That's fine." Emily wasn't particularly hungry, but she'd ordered stuffed mushrooms, hoping to give herself something to do. She'd never been to a bar by herself, let alone a dusky little lounge connected to a midpriced motel.

Of course, it certainly beat holing up in her room, worrying herself into the ground.

As the waitress departed, Emily glanced at the stranger again. But when he turned in her direction, time stopped, the earth freezing on its axis.

Their gazes met and held, like magnets to metal.

Spellbound, neither blinked. Neither broke the bond. They simply stared at each other from across the room.

Emily's mouth went dry. Within an instant, within one heart-palpitating moment, he'd left her breathless.

He wasn't flirting, she thought. It was more than that. Much more. He watched her with masculine recognition, as if he knew what it was like to touch her, to hold her, to run his hands over every inch of her body.

Dear God.

Determined to regain her composure, to sever the nerve-jangling tie, she lifted her wine and took a small sip, but her fingers quaked around the glass.

What would he think if he knew she had cancer? Would he still be looking at her with longing in his eyes?

Don't dwell on that, her subconscious warned. No self-pity. No fear. She wasn't dying. Sooner or later, the cancer would be gone.

And so would a portion of her skin.

The song on the jukebox ended and another began. This time, an early Elvis tune played havoc with her emotions. Another favored melody, she thought. Another connection to the mysterious stranger.

Did he live in this area? Or had he come to Lewiston to see family members? To meet up with an old friend?

Emily had come here for an appointment at a medical center located ninety minutes from home. She could have made the trip in one day, but she'd decided to stay the night, to reflect, to spend some time alone.

In exactly two weeks, she was scheduled for a wide excision, a surgery that would cut away the cancer. At this point, two weeks seemed like an eternity, but her condition, the melanoma, wouldn't progress in fourteen days. It wasn't an unreasonable amount of time, not between insurance authorizations and the surgeon's availability.

Emily took a deep breath. She'd promised herself that she wouldn't panic about going under the knife, that she wouldn't worry if the cancer had spread to her lymph nodes.

When the appetizer arrived, Meg hovered for a moment, her teased-and-sprayed hairdo bobbing as she moved her head.

"Gorgeous, isn't he?" she said.

"Yes." Emily knew the man continued to watch her. She could feel the heat of his gaze.

"Why don't you buy him a drink?"

"What?" She stared at the brazen redhead.

The waitress cocked her hip. "A beer, darlin'. He's about due for another."

"This probably isn't the best time for me to—" She paused, realizing what she was about to admit. How inadequate she felt, how disjointed.

"That's okay. It was just a suggestion." Meg gave her a friendly smile and retreated, leaving Emily alone with her thoughts.

Should she buy him a drink? Her? The small-town girl diagnosed with skin cancer?

As he finished the last of his beer, Emily lifted her fork, skewered a mushroom and sucked it into her mouth. He pushed his hair away from his forehead, exposing a widow's peak and slashing black brows.

Her entire body went woozy and warm.

To hell with the cancer. She was going to meet this man. Say something to him.

With as much courage as she could muster, she rose, determined to approach his table. As she crossed the room, she spotted Meg leaning against a barstool. She gazed at the other woman, hoping for a boost of encouragement.

The waitress flashed a sly wink.

By the time Emily reached him, her pulse thudded in her ears. He came to his feet, and she realized how tall he actually was. He towered over her by nearly a foot.

She extended a clammy palm. "My name is Emily."

He took her hand, much too easily.

"I'm James." His gaze roamed her body, up and down, over the ruffled silk blouse she'd ordered from a fancy catalog to the simple, five-pocket jeans she'd acquired at a discount store. "Dalton," he added, his voice tinged with an unrecognizable accent. "James Dalton."

Doing her darnedest to breathe, to keep a steady flow of oxygen filtering in and out of her lungs, she motioned to her table. "Would you care to join me?"

He didn't respond. Instead he reached behind her and undid the gold barrette that secured her ponytail.

Spellbound, Emily merely stood, her long, wavy hair spilling over her shoulders. She knew Meg was watching, equally bewitched by James's bold behavior.

He hooked the ornament onto his jacket pocket as if he meant to keep it. "I like the color of your hair," he said. "It reminds me of..."

Her heart leaped for her throat. "Of what?"

"Someone I used to know."

His expression turned dark, and she realized he'd yet to smile. The eyes that had been studying her seemed haunted, and his golden brown skin wore a shadow of beard stubble.

But he was still beautiful, even more enchanting up close. A jagged scar interrupted the pattern of his right eyebrow, and a slight cleft indented his chin. His cheekbones, she noticed, slashed like twin blades, balancing an Anglo versus Indian heritage. Was he from the Nez Perce reservation? Was that the reason he was in Lewiston?

He moved closer, and a shiver streaked up her spine. How would it feel to immortalize him? she wondered. To create his image on canvas?

Emily made her living waiting tables at her hometown diner, filling coffee cups and chatting with people she'd known all her life, but she dabbled in art, selling her work at weekend craft fairs. She wasn't aspiring to be more than she was. She simply enjoyed having a hobby, painting faces that fascinated her.

"Dance with me," he said.

She blinked, felt his fingers slide through her hair. "There's no dance floor."

"But there's music."

Yes, she thought. Music he'd chosen. "Meg said I should buy you a drink."

He combed through the strands, separating each wave. "Meg?"

"The waitress." Did he know he was seducing her? He must be part wizard, part warrior, part wolf—the hero of a magic tale.

"Dance with me," he said again.

She should have told him no. She should have walked away. Because somewhere deep down, she knew where this was leading. When the evening ended, James Dalton would ask for more than a dance. He no doubt wanted a warm, willing blonde to share his bed, a one-night stand, a moonlit affair to satisfy his needs.

But even so, she allowed him to take her hand, to guide her to a cozy little spot near the jukebox.

Emily had needs, too. Needs that had remained dormant for much too long. She deserved to feel whole, to see desire on a man's face, to know that he wanted her.

Especially now.

She didn't want to think about her responsibilities, even though her mind drifted to her six-year-old brother Corey, to the little boy she'd left with an overnight baby-sitter.

She'd called Corey earlier, and he'd chattered gleefully on the phone. But he didn't know that his sister was—

"Emily." James said her name, and she looked up, relinquishing her thoughts, giving him her undivided attention.

He took her into his arms, and she clung to his shoulders. Such strong shoulders, she thought. So broad. So capable.

Emily and her partner swayed to the music, moving to a slow, rhythmic song. His heart pounded against hers, the sound melding into one dizzying chant.

"They're watching us," she said. Meg, the bartender, the other patrons in the bar. She knew they were observing every fluid motion, every satin-draped pulse.

He lowered his head to nuzzle, to brush her cheek with his. His beard stubble abraded her skin, marking her with his touch.

"Can you blame them?" he asked.

"No." She couldn't blame their audience. Nor could she blame herself. Heaven help her, but James Dalton was impossible to resist.

When he cupped her face to kiss her, she leaned into him. He didn't invade her with his tongue. Covering her mouth, he sipped gently, offering a persuasive promise of what was yet to come.

He tasted of warmth, of beer, of secret liaisons, of a night she would never forget.

The kiss ended, and they stepped back to look at each other. His eyes were still haunted, still ghostly somehow, and she wondered how a tortured soul could be so beautiful.

He reached for her hair again, taking possession, confusing her even more.

Emily prided herself on being a good girl. She valued right from wrong, yet here she was, prepared to sleep with a stranger, hoping, praying that he would lead her astray.

They were an unholy combination, she thought. She reminded him of someone from his past, and he was like no one she'd ever met before.

No one at all.

James rubbed Emily's cheek with his thumb, soothing the abrasion he'd left on her skin. She was so pretty, he thought. So soft. So dangerous.

When she wet her lips, he kissed her again, only this time he used his tongue, his teeth, his entire mouth to devour her.

Greedy, hungry, desperate for more, he dragged her against his body. Her breath rushed into his, warm and silky, like the wind on a summer night. He closed his eyes, absorbing her texture, her scent, the thickness of her hair wrapped around his hands.

He'd promised himself that he wouldn't do this. That he wouldn't stalk the local bars for sex. Yet he'd done it. He'd found a soft, sweet blonde on his first night in Idaho, the first night he was free. From prison. From the equally sequestered weeks that followed.

She made a throaty sound, and he realized he didn't even know her last name. But somehow that didn't matter. In his mind, she could be Beverly.

His lover. His friend. His wife.

James opened his eyes and broke the kiss. Emily stepped back and gulped some air. She looked ravished, and much too willing to be taken again.

"I'm not seducing you," he said.

She smoothed her hair, calming the strands he'd tousled. "You're not?"

"No. It's you who's seducing me. And you're good at it." Damn good. He would make love to her here, right now, in a dark corner of the bar if he thought he could get away with it.

"You're teasing me, right?"

No, he wasn't joking, not in the least. From the instant, the very moment he'd laid eyes on Emily, he'd thought about his wife. How much he'd loved her, how much he missed her.

"Are you still interested in buying me a drink?" he asked, giving her the opportunity to change her mind, to walk away from this twisted game.

She wasn't Beverly. And he wasn't James Dalton, even if that was the identity the government had given him. His real name was Reed Blackwood, and he was an ex-con, a former mobster, an accessory to murder and a thief.

But those were his secrets. The burden of his sins.

"Yes," she said.

"Yes?" he parroted.

"I'm still interested in buying you a drink."

They proceeded to Emily's table, where he ordered a beer. The waitress didn't say anything about the sexy scene he'd caused, but she managed to slant him a Sister Mary Redhead look. Suddenly the brassy server was behaving like a nun.

James blew out a rough breath. Should he defend himself? Or would vouching for his own rotten character only earn him another spot in hell?

He turned to Emily. "She's worried about you."

"Who?"

"The waitress."

She lifted her wine, took a small sip. The glass was still half-full. "But she encouraged me to meet you."

"I know. But she's having second thoughts." He kept his hands still even if his pulse wasn't quite steady. "I guess she hadn't expected me to be so…aggressive.'' To paw Emily in public, to jam his tongue down her throat and swallow her saliva. A sex-and-sugar flavor, he thought. A sweetness men craved.

Emily gazed at him with emerald-colored eyes. Beverly's eyes had been green, too, as clear as the jewels he used to steal.

James shifted in his chair. Did she know how tempting she was?

She chewed her lip, peeling away the pale pink color, the barely-there gloss. With her heart-shaped face, fair complexion and long, sweeping lashes, she looked innocent, much too delicate to be messing around with someone like him.

''I won't hurt you,'' he heard himself say.

She moved closer. ''I won't hurt you, either.''

''Really?'' Touched by her tenderness, he almost smiled. ''You mean you're not a wacko? A female serial killer who preys on gullible guys in bars?''

She laughed, and the light, natural sound made him yearn for his wife. Unable to help himself, he grazed Emily's cheek, wishing he could kiss her again.

The redhead brought his beer. Guilty, he dropped his hand and let Emily pay for his drink.

''The next round is on me,'' he said.

The next round came an hour later, and by that time the lounge was empty. James and Emily were the only customers left.

Stumbling through a conversation, they talked about movies and music and things that hardly mattered. He'd been tempted to ask her to dance again, but decided that remaining at the table, pretending to get to know her, would make their upcoming union seem a bit more proper.

"Are you staying at the motel?" Emily asked.

"Yes. Are you?"

She nodded. "I have a room upstairs."

He wondered whose bed they would make love in. Hers, he hoped. He didn't want to alert the man in the room next to him that he'd picked up a woman in the bar. The WITSEC inspector had warned him, albeit jokingly, to stay out of trouble for at least one night.

Then, again, he wasn't breaking any rules. The Witness Security Program didn't stop their members from engaging in consensual sex.

James pulled on his beer. Emily would agree to sleep with him, wouldn't she?

Of course she would. She wasn't as innocent as she looked.

"When are you leaving?" she asked.

He set the bottle down. "Tomorrow."

"Me, too." She finished her second glass of wine. "Are you going home from here?"

He tried not to frown. Home? He hadn't had a home in ages. He'd spent a year and a half on the run from Beverly's crime lord father, the following year in a secured unit of a federal prison, testifying against the mob and serving time for his involvement in a hit that still haunted him. From there he'd spent two weeks at a safe-site orientation center, being briefed about his new identity and his relocation to Idaho.

"James?" Emily pressed.

"What? Oh, yeah. I'm going home. First thing in the morning." To a place he'd never been.

"So am I."

He didn't ask where she lived. He didn't want to know. James Dalton wasn't comfortable with small talk. And neither was Reed Blackwood. Both men had plenty to hide.

"Where are you from?" she asked before he could change the subject.

He offered up a lie, relying on the background WITSEC had created for him. "I was born in Oklahoma, but I moved a lot." Refusing to let the conversation go any further, he indicated the redhead, who thumbed through her receipts, then the bartender, who appeared to be stocking his station. "Looks like they're getting ready to close. We better head out."

James left a tip and escorted Emily to the door. He could feel the waitress watching them. He wanted to tell her that he would be good to Emily, that she was his salvation, the companion he needed for one lost lonely night, but he couldn't say something like that out loud. So he glanced over his shoulder and caught the redhead's eye, letting her know he was aware of her concern.

Outside, the night air sent a cool breeze blowing. James slipped his arm around Emily. They walked in the direction of the motel, then stopped beneath a stairwell.

"Well?" he said.

"Well?" she repeated, gazing up at him, her hair tumbling around her face.

He pressed his mouth to her ear, anxious to get closer. "Are you going to invite me to your room?"

She nodded, then turned to kiss him.

James went hard. Instantly hard.

She sighed, and he imagined licking her like a lemon drop and watching her melt against his tongue. She tasted like desire, his and hers, swirling in warm, wet—

Cursing his stupidity, he stepped back. He didn't have any condoms.

"I goofed," he said.

"What?"

"I have to get protection." He motioned to the convenience store across the street.

Her voice turned shy. "I think I'd prefer to wait in my room."

"I'll walk you." Her room was located at the top of the second set of stairs. They leaned against the door and kissed, almost too aroused to separate.

She bumped his fly, and he had the notion to forget the damn condoms, to take a chance, to have unprotected sex.

But he knew better. He'd already fathered a child he couldn't keep, a beautiful little boy he missed with all his heart. He wasn't about to make a baby with a stranger, to leave her swollen with his seed.

He smoothed a strand of hair from her cheek. "I'll be back as soon as I can."

''I'll be waiting.'' She gave him a sweet smile and unlocked her door, using the key card.

He watched her disappear, then turned to leave, thinking this was a hell of a way for Reed Blackwood to start over, to begin his life in the guise of James Matthew Dalton.

Two

Emily waited in her room, trying not to pace. Suddenly she was nervous, scared out of her inexperienced wits.

Should she tell him?

Tell him what? That she was scheduled for surgery in two weeks?

She sat on the edge of the bed and wrung her hands together. The melanoma would send him packing, that much she was sure. What hot-blooded American male would want to discuss skin cancer before sex?

Surely he wouldn't notice the mark on the back of her leg, the site where a mole had been removed. Of course not. Why would he notice a small, seemingly insignificant scar? It wouldn't matter to him.

Okay, fine. Then what about her virginity? Should

she broach that subject? Should she admit that she'd never been with anyone before?

Emily had talked to her girlfriends about their first times. They'd sipped sodas, munched on potato chips and discussed indecent details, the way women often did. But at the moment, that didn't help.

She had expected her first lover to be her only lover, the man she married, the man who would father her children. But waiting for Mr. Right seemed foolish now.

The cancer had changed her perspective. Life was too unpredictable to plan, and James Dalton was too handsome, too stirring, too erotic to ignore.

Desperate to relax, she removed her boots, peeled off her socks and looked around.

The motel room was spotless, aside from the makeup bag she'd left on the vanity and a blue T-shirt peeking out of a toppled gray suitcase.

Would James stay the night? Would he shower in her tub? Would he—

A knock sounded, and Emily nearly flew off the bed. With a deep, shaky breath, she stood, smoothed her blouse and answered the summons.

James offered a smile, an expression that gentled his rawboned features and softened the dark, hollow haunting in his eyes.

"Hi," he said.

"Hi." She stepped back and allowed him entrance into the room, her heart beating with a girlish flutter.

She locked the door, and he held up the brown paper bag in his hand. "I got 'em."

Yes, of course, she thought. The protection. He was

responsible enough to practice sex safe and experienced enough to sight the topic ahead of time. But the fact that he didn't keep condoms in his wallet set her mind at ease.

Apparently James didn't make a habit of one-nighters, of picking up women in bars.

"You still have your clothes on," he said, his smile tilting one corner of his mouth.

Her pulse leaped like a lizard. "You expected me to be naked?"

He tossed the condoms on the nightstand. "A guy can hope."

"I took off my boots," she said, almost wincing at her own naiveté, her inability to say something provocative.

He glanced at her feet. "Then you're one step ahead of me." Without hesitation, he sat on the edge of the bed, yanked off his battered boots and placed his socks inside them. "Now we're even."

"You're wearing a jacket," she pointed out.

He shrugged out of the denim and tossed it aside. "Not anymore."

Emily hadn't expected him to initiate a game, to bait her into a striptease.

Nervous, she remained near the dresser, the unit that doubled as an entertainment center.

He pushed his hair off his forehead, where the thick, dark strands routinely fell. "Your turn, pretty lady."

She didn't feel pretty, not with the lights blaring, not with him watching every move she made. Would he think her breasts were too small? Her tummy too soft? "You go next."

"That's cheating."

She moved a little closer, determined to relax, to let this happen on her terms. "My room. My rules."

"You got me there." He reached for his shirt and pulled it over his head, revealing his chest and the silver ring that pierced his left nipple.

Stunned, she stared at the shimmering ornament and noticed a black stone in the center.

"I did it a long time ago," he said.

"You pierced it yourself?"

"It was sort of a spiritual thing."

To Emily, it looked more sexual than spiritual, but she wasn't about to say that. "Is it sensitive?"

He glanced up and grinned. "Want to come closer and find out?"

Yes, she thought. She did. She couldn't believe how alluring he was. Or how incredibly dangerous he looked, half-naked on her bed, teasing her with a flirtatious smile.

He held out his hand, beckoning her. She stepped forward, and he pulled her onto the bed, kissing her hard and fast, pushing his tongue into her mouth.

Suddenly his hands were everywhere. She'd meant to turn out the bedside lamp, to ease into his arms, but he was too anxious, too hungry, too strong and muscular.

"Tell me what you like," he whispered, licking the shell of her ear, opening the top of her blouse. "Tell me what you want me to do."

Heaven help her, but she didn't know. She didn't—

"I'll do anything, Emily. Anything you want."

She had to warn him to slow down, to give her a chance to catch up. She couldn't give him directions, say the naughty things he expected to hear.

Scraping her nail across his chest, she paused at his left nipple, almost touching the captivating ring.

"I'm new at this," she said.

He lifted his head. She was pinned beneath him, the weight of his body pressing her onto the bed.

"New at what?"

"Sex. Making love. This is my first time."

His features went still, much too still. Then the scar across his eyebrow twitched. Emily held her breath. Her fingers brushed the piercing, grazing the magic stone in the center.

He pulled back, disconnecting her hand from his skin.

"We don't have to stop, James." She glanced at his zipper, saw that he was still aroused. "Do we?"

He frowned at her. Was he angry? Confused?

"How old are you?" he asked.

She bit her lip. She could still taste him, the hard, desperate tongue thrusts he'd given her. "Twenty-two."

He gazed directly into her eyes, but his were troubled again, as haunted as a ghost-ridden night. "Why me? And why now?"

She didn't know what to say, how to explain her decision, not without mentioning the cancer. And she wasn't about to bring that up, to evoke pity, or God help her, revulsion from the man she wanted to make love with.

"I'm tired of waiting," she said.

"So you pick up some guy in a bar? That makes a hell of a lot of sense."

She wanted to argue, to fight for her right to be free, to feel whole, to lose her virginity to a tall, dark stranger. "Have you looked in the mirror lately, James? Do you have any idea how handsome you are?"

"And for that you're willing to sleep with me?" He closed his eyes, made a disbelieving face. "That's insane."

"It's only sex."

He opened his eyes. "But it shouldn't be. Not your first time. You need to keep waiting, Emily. To find the right guy."

Humiliated, she clasped the front of her blouse. He was turning her down. Her fantasy lover was walking away.

He skimmed her cheek, gently, almost too gently for her to endure. She wanted to ask him to stay, to hold her, but she didn't have the courage to bare her soul, to admit that she still needed him.

He dropped his hand. "I can't do this."

She lifted her chin, protecting her pride. "It doesn't matter."

"I have to go." He pulled his shirt over his head and reached for his boots. "If I don't leave now, I'll..." The words drifted, fading into nothingness.

Emily remained where she was, watching him. Finally, he stood, looking like the troubled warrior he was, his T-shirt catching on the top of his belt buckle.

He grabbed his jacket, and in the next instant he was gone, closing the door and leaving her alone.

Much too alone.

At 6:00 a.m. James gazed at his reflection in the mirror. When he'd agreed to enter WITSEC, he'd assumed the government would alter his features, but plastic surgery hadn't been part of the deal. His face was the same as it had always been, including the scar that cut across his eyebrow, the mark he'd acquired the first time he'd gone to prison.

Emily liked the way he looked. She'd been willing to sleep with him, to give up her virginity, because she thought he was handsome.

Disturbed by her reasoning, James studied his features. Would Emily still find him attractive if she knew he was an ex-con? An accessory to murder?

Spewing a vile curse, he turned away from the mirror. Why did she have to remind him of Beverly? He had been Beverly's first lover, the man she'd given it up for, but the circumstances were different.

Beverly Halloway had been in love with him. Emily, the lady with no last name, didn't know him from Adam.

Struggling to clear his mind, he made one last check of the room, grabbed his meager belongings and headed out the door, where the sun had already risen.

He squinted into the daylight and saw Zack Ryder, the field inspector assigned to his case, leaning against his car. James didn't have a vehicle, but

WITSEC had provided him with enough money to purchase a used pickup once he got settled.

Ryder drew on a dwindling cigarette and blew a stream of smoke into the air. "'Morning.''

James merely nodded. Ryder was a mixed-blood, part Indian like himself, tall and strongly built, but that was where the similarity ended. The inspector looked about forty, with graying temples and a sardonic sense of humor.

He belonged to an elite unit of the U.S. Marshal Service and was trained to protect more than witnesses. Foreign dignitaries and government officials had probably crossed his path, as well.

James, on the other hand, was only twenty-six and had spent most of his youth learning to be a criminal. Boasting a genius IQ, he was a self-taught electronics expert, capable of deactivating the most sophisticated security systems ever designed. In his spare time, he used to build countersurveillance equipment. Skills, naturally, the mob had admired. It hadn't taken him long to become a "made" man, a soldier in the Los Angeles-based West Coast Family.

Ryder motioned to the restaurant affiliated with the motel. "Ready for some chow?"

James adjusted the bag over his shoulder. "That's the last place I want to eat."

"Why? Does it have roaches I don't know about?"

"I just want to get on the road." And avoid running into Emily. What if she decided to have breakfast here? He glanced down the row of cars and spotted the compact he suspected was hers.

"How about McDonald's?" Ryder asked.

"As long as we're driving through." James didn't want to linger in Lewiston. He wanted to forget this town, forget that he'd met Emily here. He'd tossed and turned half the night, thinking about her, wondering who she was, where she lived.

He wasn't supposed to care, but he was worried about the next guy she met in a bar, worried the bastard would be all too willing to take what she offered.

Ryder unlocked his sedan, got behind the wheel and snuffed out his cigarette in the ashtray. When he opened the trunk, James stowed his bag and climbed into the car.

While they drank coffee and ate Egg McMuffins, James leaned back in his seat. WITSEC had decided to relocate him to Silver Wolf, a small town in North Central Idaho, positioned about an hour and a half from Lewiston.

Ryder drove with one hand, his sandwich in the other. "You might want to check out Tandy Stables."

"What for?"

"A job. The old lady who runs the place is looking for an assistant. The position comes with room and board, a mobile home on her property."

"How do you know?"

The inspector inclined his head. "I made it my business to know. Did you think I'd dump you in a small town with no job prospects? Besides, I heard you're good with horses."

James shrugged. He'd grown up in the Texas Hill Country, riding and roping and playing cowboy. Or outlaw, he supposed. "I've spent as much time in the country as the city."

"Then getting back to basics will do you some good. Speaking of which—" Ryder slanted him a wary-eyed glance "—you look like hell, Dalton."

"I didn't get much sleep."

"Why not? Too busy jumping some pretty blonde in the bar?"

Son of a bitch. The deputy marshal knew exactly what had gone down. "I didn't break any rules."

"Yeah, well, the first time you do, I'll come gunning for your ass. We'll kick you out of this program faster than you picked up on that blonde."

"Leave her out of this." The last thing James wanted was to talk about Emily, to admit that she'd gotten under his skin.

The inspector shoved his sandwich wrapper into the empty food bag. "Just don't screw up." He flashed a peace-treaty smile, letting James know he was more friend than foe. "You'll make me look bad."

"I don't plan on screwing up." But ex-cons never did, he supposed. He couldn't blame Ryder for being skeptical. But, then, the inspector didn't know the whole story. No one, not even WITSEC or the FBI knew that James had fathered a child, a dark-haired, dark-eyed boy he'd asked another man to claim. In his heart, James was different. Being a parent, even a secret one, had changed him.

Ninety minutes later Ryder turned off the highway and onto a small country road. "This is it."

James looked out the window, noting the tall timbers and quaint wooden buildings. WITSEC had showed him videos of Silver Wolf, familiarizing him with the area. They'd debated sending him to a Cher-okee community, but were concerned the mob would expect him to seek sanctuary among his tribe. So they'd picked a place near the Nez Perce reservation, an Indian Nation he wasn't connected to.

The inspector parked in front of the Silver Wolf Lodge. James gazed at the shrub-shrouded motel, knowing this was his temporary home. Once he landed a job, possibly the position Ryder mentioned, he would acquire a permanent place to live.

From there, WITSEC would expect him to estab-lish roots, to blend in. Unless, of course, his security was breached and he had to be relocated again.

Three days had passed since that night in Lewiston, since Emily had lost her fantasy lover. Enough time to forget, to move on, yet she couldn't seem to get her harried life in order.

Dashing into the back room of Dolly's All-Night Diner, she punched her time card.

"I'm sorry I'm late," she said to the graveyard-shift waitress waiting to leave. "I had a meeting at Corey's school and it ran longer than I expected."

"That's all right. We've all got kids," came the gracious reply.

Emily sighed. She didn't have kids. She had a younger brother, a child she did her best to mother, in spite of his knack for diving headfirst into exhaust-ing doses of mischief.

She greeted the cook and took her place on the floor, scanning the diner. The place was relatively quiet, leaving her little to do.

Of course, the locals were here, as regular as clock-work. Lorna, the beautician across the street, paid the cashier for her typical take-out order, and Harvey Osborn, a retired postal worker, occupied his usual stool.

Across from Harvey, at an end booth, she spotted the back of someone's head, a man in a black cowboy hat. A newspaper was spread in front of him, taking up most of the table.

Emily turned the revolving wheel at the cook's counter, checking out the orders she'd inherited, including Harvey's cherry Danish and never-ending boost of coffee.

When she refilled his cup, he looked up and smiled. He was a bony little man, with narrow shoulders and baggy trousers. He wore striped suspenders every day, but she suspected he needed them to hold up his pants.

"How are you, missy?" he asked.

"Fine." Harvey, of course, knew about her cancer. He made a point of knowing everyone's business, of gossiping like a blue-haired matron.

Keeping his voice low, he cocked his head toward the man in the black hat. "I'll bet he's Lily Mae's new assistant."

"You think so?" Harvey loved to talk about Lily Mae Prescott, the scatterbrained proprietor of Tandy Stables.

He nudged her arm. "Why don't you go find out?"

"I suppose I should say hello. Let him know his order is almost ready." She turned, coffeepot in hand, and approached the black hat.

The man shifted, rattled the paper and looked up.

Emily nearly dropped the glass carafe. "James?"

There he was, as rough and rugged as the timeworn Stetson shielding his eyes, as dark and forbidden as her dreams, as the ache of not making love with him.

She feared she might faint.

"Emily?" Equally stunned, he stared at her.

She moved forward, battling for composure, pretending to do her job. "Do you want more coffee?"

"No. Yes. I guess so."

He made no sense, but she understood his confusion. They'd never expected to see each other again.

She poured the hot brew, filling his cup, telling herself she would survive this incredibly awkward moment, the pounding of her heart, the ringing in her ears.

His jaw, she noticed, was clean shaven, scraped free of the dark stubble. But somehow, he still managed to look like a desperado, an Indian renegade.

"I thought you were going home," she said, her voice as unsteady as her pulse.

"I am home. I just moved here."

Oh, God. Dear God.

"That's why I was in Lewiston." He cleared his throat, attempted to explain. "I flew in that night. The motel was close to the airport. It was convenient." He lifted his cup, set it back down. "Why were you there?"

"I—" She set the coffeepot on his table. "I had an appointment that afternoon, and I didn't feel like driving home."

"So you got a room?"

"Yes." He seemed like a mirage, a figment of her

tortured imagination, but he was real. Heaven help her. He was real.

"I didn't mean for this to happen, Emily."

"It's okay. It's fine." She wiped her clammy hands on her uniform, on the pink dress she routinely wore. "You'll like this town."

"Geez, Louise," Harvey said from behind her. "You two young folks know each other?"

Silent, James shifted his gaze to the old-timer. Harvey moseyed on over, shuffling his way to the booth.

Emily stood like a statue. She'd tried to forget James Dalton. She'd tried so hard, so desperately to erase him from her mind, from the memory imbedded in her soul.

Without waiting for an invitation, Harvey sat across from James. "Are you Lily Mae's new assistant?"

"Yes. She just hired me this morning."

"Hot diggity. I knew it." He turned to Emily. "Didn't I tell ya?" Then back to James. "So, how'd you meet our little Emmy? What's this about Lewiston?"

Caught off guard, James folded the paper. Emily saw him struggle to answer, to find a suitable explanation. "I noticed her. I thought she was pretty."

And he'd wanted to sleep with me, she thought. Until he'd discovered she'd never had sex before.

Harvey flashed his dentures. "I think she's pretty, too. That's why I loiter…I mean, eat here. But don't tell the other waitresses I said that. They think I hang around for them."

James's mouth, that warm, firm mouth, tilted in a faint smile, and Emily recalled the lust-driven flavor of his last kiss, the very moment he'd pulled her onto the bed.

Then let her go.

After Harvey introduced himself to Silver Wolf's newest resident, reciting his name and how long he'd lived in this county, he said, "So you'll be working with Lily Mae. That woman's crazy, you know."

"Must be why she hired me."

When James glanced her way, Emily thought about her upcoming surgery. Would he find out? Would Harvey tell him?

"I'll check on your order," she said to James, hoping to prod Harvey back to his stool.

But the gossip guru remained where he was, blabbing about Lily Mae Prescott.

Finally, when she brought James's breakfast, Harvey excused himself, pleased that he'd spoken his piece about Lily Mae.

After the older man paid his bill and left the restaurant, James lifted the brim of his hat, exposing his eyes.

Those haunted eyes.

"They must have been lovers," he said.

"What?" Emily realized she'd left the coffeepot on his table all this time. That her brain was completely addled.

"Harvey and Lily Mae."

His words sunk in. "You think he and she—"

"A long time ago. When they were young."

She blinked, stared at him, blinked again. "No one has ever assumed that before. Lily Mae drives Harvey nuts."

"Because he can't get her out of his system." James tapped on his chest. "It happens sometimes. A woman gets inside you, and you can't let her go. You—" He paused, as if suddenly aware of what he was saying, of what he was feeling.

Emily didn't know how to react. She knew he was thinking about the other blonde, the woman she reminded him of. "I better go. Let you eat your meal."

She attempted to turn away, but he stopped her.

"Wait. Emily, wait."

Her pulse jumped. "Yes?"

"You didn't...you haven't—" he stalled, reached for the ketchup "—found someone else?"

Embarrassed, she shook her head. "It wasn't that important."

His hand slid down the base of the bottle, then back up. "Wasn't it?"

"No. It was just a whim." She released the air in her lungs. Was he caressing the glass? Molding it like a woman's body?

His voice turned rough. "I just wanted to be sure that someone else didn't..."

Didn't what? Take her virginity? Make her feel good? She chewed her lip, tasting the gloss she'd applied earlier. "I have to get back to work."

She grabbed the coffeepot and left him alone, staring at the ketchup bottle in his hand.

After a short while, she returned, asking if he wanted anything else. Avoiding eye contact, he shook his head, and she put his bill on the table.

He lingered at the booth, a lone figure in dark

clothes, scattered light from a shaded window sending shadows across his face.

Other customers filtered into the diner, and Emily went about her job, taking orders, chatting with people she knew.

Later, as she balanced two breakfast specials, she scanned the room to see him, to look at him one more time. But he was gone, his bill paid, his food barely eaten.

She cleared his table and reached for the shiny gold ornament that held her tip.

It wasn't a money clip. It was her hair barrette, the one he'd hooked to his jacket on the night they should have made love.

The night he'd left her wanting more.

Three

Emily lived seven miles from town on a paved country road. Her yellow-and-white house, James noticed, looked like a cottage, something out of a gingerbread fairy tale.

He parked his newly acquired truck and sat behind the wheel, hoping the purpose of his visit wouldn't put her off. He hadn't seen her for several days, since he'd left the diner without saying goodbye. But he'd run into Harvey Osborn this afternoon at the hardware store, and the old guy had given James an earful.

So here he was, parked on her street, preparing to confront her.

A woman he barely knew.

A woman who had cancer.

He studied the decorative lamppost in front of her house, wondering if the Creator had put Emily in his path for a reason. If meeting her was part of some sort of divine plan.

Yeah, right.

Did he honestly believe the Creator gave a damn about him? That he was even worthy of a plan?

James wasn't exactly the disciple of a deity. He was an ex-con, an accessory to murder, a man who had no business associating with someone like Emily.

He cursed beneath his breath and exited his vehicle, knowing he should head back to work instead, forget about Emily, keep his distance. But he couldn't. He simply couldn't. He needed to talk to her.

Taking the shrub-lined walkway to her stoop, he adjusted his hat, shielding his eyes, guarding his emotions.

Her dome-shaped door displayed a four-paned window, but he couldn't see through the smoked glass nor could he predict what awaited him on the other side.

What was he supposed to say to her? How was he supposed to start this conversation?

James knocked, rapping softly. Within a heartbeat, within one anxious, chest-pounding thump, Emily answered the summons, and he had to remind himself to breathe.

Her hair, that honey-blond mane, waved in a loose natural style, springing softly around her face. And her eyes, as green as a sunlit meadow, caught his, trapping him beneath the battered brim of his hat.

She could have been Beverly, he thought. The lady he'd loved.

"James?"

She blinked her sweeping lashes, and he told himself she wasn't his wife. Her resemblance to Beverly wasn't that specific.

What about her illness? The disease that chilled his bones?

That, he decided, was specific enough to bring him to her door, to leave him standing here, tongue-tied and terminally tortured.

"James?" she said again.

He found his voice, raw as it was. "Harvey told me where you lived."

"I wasn't expecting company," she responded, a bit too cautiously. "I just got off work a little while ago. But I suppose Harvey mentioned that, too."

James frowned. "Why didn't you tell me you had cancer?"

Her breath rushed out, and he wondered if she'd gone woozy. She gripped the doorknob, her cheeks turning pale. "When was I supposed to tell you?"

"How about the night we met?" The hot, hungry night he'd almost made love to her.

"I couldn't."

"Why not?"

"It would have been awkward."

No more awkward than this, he thought.

She released the doorknob, but her hands didn't remain idle for long. She fidgeted with the T-shirt she wore, tugging uncomfortably at the fabric.

"It's no big deal," she said.

No big deal? He had the notion to shake her. To hold her, to drag her next to his body and never let go.

James's wife had died of lung cancer. Beverly had been as young and beautiful as Emily. As delicate. As stubborn. He knew the disease didn't discriminate. Those who weren't supposed to be at risk sometimes ended up on a grassy slope, marked by an elegant headstone, by a slab of marble etched with a lonesome epitaph.

A grave James couldn't visit. A resting place that gave him no peace.

"I want answers, Emily. I want to know about your condition."

"I thought Harvey told you."

"He didn't have all the details."

"What did he say?"

"That you have skin cancer. And you're having surgery."

She lifted her chin, gave him a tough-girl look. "That's plenty of information. More than you need to know."

"Like hell."

Her expression didn't falter. "I'm under no obligation to explain myself to you."

He moved closer, crowding her. "Five days ago you were willing to let me pop your cherry. And not because you were tired of waiting." Battling his temper, he cursed his own comment. But what did he care about being proper? About protecting the honor of a woman he barely knew? "You were freaked out about the cancer. Admit it. That's why you picked up a stranger in a bar."

"So what's your excuse?" she shot back.

My dead wife, he wanted to say. The mother of his

lost child. "Men don't need excuses. Men—" He froze, realizing how harsh he sounded, how ungentlemanly he was behaving.

God help him, he knew better. In spite of his crude upbringing, of the crimes he'd committed, he knew how to treat a lady, how to respect her.

"Men what?" she asked, shoving at his shoulder, trying in vain to push him away, to keep the monster he was at bay.

"Nothing," he said, taking a step back, giving her the space she needed, hating himself for the discomfort he saw in her eyes.

She released a shaky sigh, and he resisted the urge to spill his lowlife guts, to admit why her cancer made him crazy.

"I'm sorry, Emily."

"Are you?"

"Yes." He held up his hands, like an outlaw trying to stop the bullet he deserved. "I'm just worried about you."

She chewed on her bottom lip, a nervous habit he'd seen her do before. Was she contemplating his sincerity?

"I'll tell you what you want to know," she finally said.

Silent, he waited for her to make the next move. Which she did, by gesturing to the shallow ridge on her front stoop, offering him a place to sit.

What did he expect after the way he'd acted? For her to invite him into her home? Into her fairy-tale cottage with its lace curtains and artfully painted trim—a place someone like him would never belong.

Emily sat beside James in the shady spot she'd chosen, unsure of where to begin. Her shoulder brushed his, and the contact made her foolishly weak. She would never forget the way he'd kissed her that night, the erotic, openmouthed pressure of his lips, the wetness from his tongue.

And now he wanted to hear about her cancer.

She turned to look at him. Their faces were close. Too close. She shouldn't have suggested such tight quarters, such a confined place to have this conversation.

His eyes were nearly hidden by the brim of his hat. She couldn't see into the window of his soul, couldn't uncover his secrets. Even though he'd managed to uncover all of hers.

"Do you know anything about skin cancer?" she asked.

He shook his head. "A little. But not enough to understand what's happening to you."

"I have melanoma." The most dangerous form of skin cancer, she thought. "It begins in a type of cell called a melanocyte. Melanocyctes produce melanin."

"The pigment in our skin," he said.

"Yes." She gazed at him, at his deep, rich coloring. "People with fair skin and red or blond hair are at risk because their skin cells have less melanin."

"Like you."

She nodded. In spite of her fair skin, of her tendency to burn, she'd spent years trying to perfect a tan, to look good in a bathing suit. She thrived on summer days, on splashing in a nearby river, on strolling along sun-dappled trails.

Until now.

"How did you find out you had melanoma?" he asked.

"I went to my HMO doctor on another matter. I twisted my ankle and decided to have it x-rayed." Avoiding his gaze, she glanced at the yard. A freshly fallen leaf stirred in the breeze, fluttering to the ground. The May weather was mild, but Emily's emotions ran rampant. She dreaded the onset of summer, of challenging the sun, of being overly cautious every time she stepped outside. "My ankle was fine, but the doctor noticed a suspicious-looking mole on my leg."

"Suspicious-looking?"

"The shape was irregular and the color was uneven. I never paid much attention to it. To me, it was just a mole. It had been there for years." Emily steadied her voice, determined to make this sound more clinical. Less personal. She wanted to overcome her anxiety, to feel like herself again. "My doctor referred me to a skin care clinic in Lewiston. They removed the mole and got a pathology report."

He waited for her to continue, but she paused to pull air into her lungs. She didn't like discussing this with a stranger, a man she'd almost slept with.

He shifted his weight, making her much too aware of his body next to hers. Anxious to get this conversation over with, she went on. "There are different types of melanoma and the disease is diagnosed in stages, which is determined by the thickness of the cancer and how deeply it's invaded the skin. Mine is considered stage one.''

''When is your surgery scheduled?''

Rather than gesture to the afflicted area, to the part of her that would soon be scarred, she kept her hands still. ''Next Friday.''

James studied her, much too intensely. ''What about recovery time?''

''It depends on the extent of your surgery and what kind of work you do. I'm taking a month off.'' She wondered why he seemed determined to grill her, to acquire every last detail. ''My boss offered me a few weeks sick pay, and I was going to take a vacation this summer anyway.'' To spend some lazy days at the river, she thought. To bask in the sun. Something she could no longer do. ''That will be more than enough time.''

''Is your family going to look after you?''

''My parents passed away.''

''I'm sorry,'' he said, his shadowed eyes meeting hers.

''Thank you.'' Facing this without her mom and dad made her feel vulnerable, especially with James watching her so closely.

He cleared his throat and prompted her with another question. ''Who's taking you to the hospital?''

''A girlfriend. She's going to keep an eye on me afterward, too.''

''I can help,'' he said. ''I can stop by when your friend isn't available.''

She shook her head. ''I'll be fine.''

"Are you sure?" He reached out to skim her cheek, to trace the contours of her face.

"Yes." Emily refused to admit how nervous she was, how being diagnosed with cancer had changed her. "I won't be bedridden."

He ran his fingers along her jaw. "If you need me, all you have to do is call."

She took a deep breath. Her skin tingled from his touch, sending little shivers along her spine.

"I'll give you my number," he said.

"That isn't necessary."

"Just in case." He reached into his shirt pocket and handed her a business card from Tandy Stables.

She glanced at it, noticed his name and number were written in the corner. Without thinking, she pressed the card against her chest, then realized his name and number were dangerously close to her heart.

They both fell silent, and a moment later, a familiar yellow bus made its way down the road, stopping where it always did. A six-year-old boy ambled out, his backpack weighing down narrow shoulders.

"My brother's home." And she'd lost track of time, forgetting about Corey, who arrived every day at this hour, twenty minutes after his after-school care program ended.

The rambunctious first-grader headed toward the house, while a female bus driver waited for him to reach the stone walkway, the red lights on her vehicle flashing.

James adjusted his hat, lifting the brim a notch. "That little tyke is your brother?"

"Yes." The fair-haired child with the gap-toothed grin belonged to her. "I'm his legal guardian." And she'd finally explained her condition to him, letting him know she couldn't play in the sun the way she used to.

She stepped forward to greet Corey, but he was more interested in the tall, dark stranger by her side.

The boy gaped at James. "Who are you?"

The man she'd almost slept with crouched down, putting himself at Corey's level. "I'm a friend of your sister's."

The six-year-old turned his gape on Emily. "You got a boyfriend, Emmy?"

Her tongue twisted in her mouth, her saliva going dry. "No...I...he..."

"I'm not her boyfriend," James supplied.

Corey dumped his backpack on the ground, changing the subject, switching to another uncomfortable topic. "Did you know Emmy's gonna have surgee?" he asked, the mispronounced word whistling through his teeth.

"Yes, she told me. Are you going to help her get better?"

"Yep. I'm gonna spend the night at Steven's house so she can rest. I'm gonna be there for four whole days."

"Is Steven your friend?"

"Uh-huh. He's got bunk beds in his room and everything." He paused to take a quick breath, then prattled on, "My name's Corey. When Emmy gets mad, she calls me Corbin. What's your name?"

"I'm James." The big man smiled, the tilt of his lips amused yet wistful.

Emily wondered what he was thinking. He seemed drawn to her brother, gently affected by the chatty youth.

"Wanna play video games with me?" Corey asked.

"I wish I could. But I have to go to work now." James pointed to his pickup, a sturdy Ford packed with lumber. "There are some repairs that need to be done at the barn."

"Are you a cowboy?" Corey wanted to know, as he checked out the western hat and battered boots.

James smiled again. "Yes, I guess I am. Do you like horses?"

"Yeah. I like 'em a lot. Can you come back to our house for dinner tonight?" Her brother spun around. "Can he, Emmy?"

Before she could respond, James rose. Suddenly his eyes, those dark, tortured eyes, caught hers. Did he want to share a meal with her and Corey?

Did it matter? Refusing to invite him to dinner would seem rude, something a properly bred, small-town girl would never do.

"It won't be anything fancy," she found herself saying, her eyes still locked on to his. "But you're welcome to join us."

"Thank you. That'd be nice." He accepted, then glanced at Corey, who gave an excited little jump.

Emily reached for her brother's backpack, praying

she'd done the right thing, that making friends with James Dalton wouldn't complicate her already complicated life.

James walked to the closet and opened the door. His new home was a nicely furnished, single-wide coach that provided plenty of comfort. Enough for a man who'd spent the past year in a prison cell.

Anxious about tonight, he scanned his clothes. Aside from a few recently purchased T-shirts, his personal belongings were in piss-poor shape.

He grabbed one of the T-shirts and cursed his unsteady nerves. This wasn't a date. He wasn't required to get gussied up, to slap on some fancy-ass cologne and tame his shower-dampened hair. Nor was he required to show up with a long-stemmed rose or a bottle of a rare-vintage wine.

No, this wasn't a date. He was simply having dinner with a woman and a child.

A woman and child who reminded him of what he'd lost.

James placed the T-shirt over his head and tucked it into a pair of fraying jeans. He fumbled with his zipper, his fingers refusing to cooperate. He shouldn't have accepted Emily's invitation. But he couldn't cancel. Not now. Dinner had been Corey's idea and he couldn't bear to disappoint the boy.

He headed for the bathroom and dragged a comb through his hair. Most kids were wary of him, distrustful of his hard, dark, don't-screw-with-me looks. But not Emily's brother. Corey had grinned at him, flashing a warm, genuine smile.

So go. Get going. Be on time for dinner.

He grabbed his keys, then decided that showing up empty-handed would make him feel like an ill-mannered oaf.

On his way to Emily's house, he stopped by the supermarket in town and bought a cellophane-wrapped bouquet of flowers and a toy car.

He arrived on her cozy stoop, reminding himself that this wasn't a date. But when she answered the door wearing a pretty spring blouse and a hint of perfume, he wanted to kiss her, cover her mouth with his and taste all that feminine beauty.

"Hi," she said.

"Hi." He handed her the flowers.

"Thank you." She sniffed a protruding daisy and invited him inside. "Corey fell asleep. He wore himself out waiting for you. But I'll wake him before dinner."

"Oh. Okay." James fidgeted with the toy car. Emily's house was bright and cheerful, with wood floors, colorful area rugs and wicker furniture. It still reminded him of a gingerbread cottage, of a fairy-tale dwelling.

He spotted her brother sacked out on the couch, and without the slightest hesitation, he ventured toward the boy.

Corey didn't look anything like James's son. They weren't even near the same age. Yet he couldn't help but think about his lost child.

Justin was only ten months old the last time James had seen him. By now the boy would be walking, talking, calling another man Daddy.

"Kids look so sweet when they're asleep," he said,

recalling the nights he used to rock Justin, hum lullabies while taking refuge in cars, motels and campgrounds. His son had been born during the year and a half he, his wife and sister had been on the run from the mob.

He turned to glance at Emily and saw that she watched him. Closely. Much too closely.

Feigning a casual air, he set the racy red car on the coffee table. ''Not that I know anything about kids.''

Emily still held the supermarket bouquet, the arrangement of yellow, pink and lavender blooms. ''Corey certainly likes you.''

He resisted the notion to smooth the child's hair, to brush his bangs from his eyes. ''I like him, too.''

When their conversation fell short, he jammed his hands into his pockets, and she hugged the flowers to her chest.

''Do you need any help with dinner?'' he asked.

She blinked, let out an audible breath. ''Can you cook?''

He managed a halfhearted smile. ''A little bit. Enough to get by.''

''Then follow me.''

Her cluttered yet functional kitchen offered wind chimes in the window, eclectic canisters on the counter and an appetite-stirring aroma.

''What's in the oven?'' he asked.

''A roast.'' She unwrapped the bouquet and arranged it in a rainbow-colored vase.

He glanced at the glass-topped table, which had already been set with green-and-yellow plates, and noticed a portrait of an aging gypsy on the wall.

James approached the bejeweled woman, then stopped to study her. Her reddish-brown hair glistened with streaks of silver and the shawl around her shoulders shimmered like a belly dancer's veil. A deck of tarot cards lay just below her gnarled, liver-spotted hands. But it was her eyes that held the most power. The eyes of a crow, he thought.

Emily moved to stand beside him. "That's Madam Myra. She came through town, traveling with a run-down carnival."

"She's fascinating," James said.

"I thought so, too. That's why I asked her to sit for me."

Stunned, he turned to look at her. "You painted this?"

"It's just a hobby."

"No." He shook his head. "It's more than that. It's part of who you are."

She met his gaze, and for a long, soundless moment, they stared at each other. The way they'd done before, on the first night they'd met. Suddenly James couldn't see anything but Emily, couldn't feel anything but her presence, the magic that consumed him.

"Madam Myra gave me a reading," she said. "But I didn't think it was real."

"Why? What did she tell you?"

"That I was—" She paused, took a breath. "Going to meet a tall, dark stranger. But that's such a cliché. It's—"

Once again, they stared at each other, the gypsy's reading hovering in the air, swirling around James like a familiar verse from an ancient Cherokee spell.

A spell of attraction, he thought. Of enchantment, of following a path that was meant to be.

Maybe the Creator *had* sent James to Silver Wolf. To Emily. To a woman struggling with cancer, a disease that had killed his wife.

She continued to gaze at him, leaving him with a hunger in his heart and an incantation playing like a poem in his head.

"I want to take you to the hospital," he said. "I want to be there when you have your surgery."

"What? No." She broke eye contact and stepped back.

"Then I want to see you the next day. You have to promise to call, to let me come by as soon as you get home."

"Why, James? Why does it matter?"

Because of the spell, he thought. The magic. The crow-eyed gypsy. "Because I need to know that you'll be okay. And you need—"

"What?" she asked. "What do I need?"

"Me," he told her, his voice turning raw. "You need me."

Four

Emily's heartbeat blasted her chest. "No," she said, fighting his comment. "I needed you last week, James." She'd needed him at the motel. But she didn't need him now, not like this, not on the heels of discussing her cancer.

He moved closer, and she feared he would touch her. She couldn't think straight when he put his hands on her, when he caressed her face, combed his fingers through her hair.

"Last week wasn't the right time, Emily. You weren't ready for a lover."

"I don't want to talk about this."

He moved closer still, nearly pinning her against the counter. "Why? Because it scares you? Because you know I'm right?"

Right about what? Needing him? Or not being

ready for a lover? "You're confusing me." If she needed him, then she needed him as a lover, not as a nursemaid.

He looked so big, so tall, so strong. And now, God help her, she wanted him to touch her, to put those rough, calloused hands all over her.

"Just call me, okay? Call me after you get home from your surgery."

No, she thought. No. She wouldn't involve him in her recovery. That would destroy the sexuality between them, the spark that drew him to her.

The spark that jumbled her emotions.

"I have to check on the roast," she said, changing the subject, searching for a way out.

He stepped back, and she noticed the discomfort in his eyes. If only she could make him understand why she didn't want him fussing over her surgery.

"What do you want me to do?" he asked.

Emily merely stared. "About what?"

"The meal. How can I help?"

She let out the breath she'd been holding and motioned to the refrigerator, where her brother's artwork was displayed. "You can make the salad. The lettuce is in the crisper and the tomatoes are in a bowl on the other side of the counter."

"What about a colander? To clean the lettuce?"

She opened a cabinet and handed it to him, and in the process, they both froze. His fingers brushed hers, a light, barely-there touch that shouldn't have mattered. Yet it did.

Who was he? she wondered. Who was this stranger who sent shockwaves through her system?

For a moment, neither moved. Then he turned to the sink, and she opened the oven and poked at the roast.

Corey stumbled into the kitchen, sleepy-eyed from his nap and carrying the toy James had brought him. Emily was grateful for his presence. He lightened James's mood right away, making the troubled cowboy smile.

"Hey, partner," he said to the boy.

"Hi. Is this from you?"

"Yes. It's a Ferrari. One of my favorite cars."

"Mine, too," Corey said, although Emily was certain he'd never heard of the Italian sports car.

James shifted to look at her, and she suspected he knew Corey was bluffing. But he didn't seem to mind. If anything, he seemed flattered by the boy's attention, by the innocence of the six-year-old's idol worship.

Corey moved to stand beside James, running his new toy up and down the counter, making engine noises. Emily prepared cream peas to go along with the rest of the meal, the roast and potatoes and carrots she'd seasoned with familiar spices. She couldn't recall the last time she'd had a man in her kitchen. Corey probably couldn't remember, either.

Soon the boy stopped revving his Ferrari and looked up at James, who tore lettuce leaves into a bowl. "Emmy thinks you're part Indian."

James glanced her way, then turned back to Corey. "Emmy's right."

"Are you from the Nose Pierce tribe?"

James cracked a smile. "You mean Nez Perce?"

He dried his hands, giving Corey his undivided attention. "No. I'm Cherokee."

Emily wanted to interject, but she remained quiet, observing James and her brother, listening to their conversation. She'd assumed James was from the Nez Perce Nation, too.

"What's Cherokee?" the child asked.

"It's a different kind of Indian."

"Oh."

Corey seemed disappointed, but Emily knew he'd learned about the Nez Perce in school, even if their French-given name eluded him. When she'd taken him on a shopping outing in Lewiston, he'd oohed and awed over the life-size bronze of a Nez Perce man on horseback in front of the county courthouse.

"Did the Cherokee wear those big feather things on their heads?" Corey asked.

James shook his head. "No. But sometimes the men wore cloth turbans, and Cherokee boys were tattooed at an early age, with pictures of stars and animals and things like that."

"Really?" The child spun around. "Can I get a tattoo? Please, Emmy. Can I?"

Good Lord. She glanced at James, hoping he'd intercede, but he merely shrugged, letting her tackle this on her own. "I suppose you have a tattoo," she said to him.

"Yep. But you'll have to guess where it is."

Corey shuffled his feet, clearly enthralled with the idea of James's mysterious tattoo. "Yeah, Emmy. Guess."

Oh, what the heck. "I'll bet it's on his butt," she said, making her brother laugh.

James laughed, too. Then raised an eyebrow at her, challenging her to guess again. But she didn't dare. Envisioning his body, the parts she'd yet to see, was a dangerous game.

Corey refused to drop the subject. "Where is your tattoo, James?"

He leaned over and lifted his right pant leg, exposing his boot and part of his calf. "It's here."

The child squinted at the design. "What is it?"

"A crow."

"How come you got that?" Corey wanted to know.

"Because crows are shape-shifters. And if you look into a crow's eye, you'll find the gateway to the supernatural. Like the gypsy in that picture. The one your sister painted."

Although the explanation seemed to confuse her brother, it sent a chill along Emily's spine.

She glanced at Madam Myra, then at James's leg. His tattoo was in the same spot where the melanoma had taken root on her body.

Emily turned away to finish the meal, but for the rest of the evening, she couldn't think straight. She barely spoke to James, barely made eye contact.

She let Corey take over, and luckily the boy chattered enough for both of them.

And when James left, when he said goodbye, she told herself that her connection to him was coincidence, that he wasn't the stranger Madam Myra had predicted. That the gypsy's reading was nonsense.

But she knew better. Whatever was happening between her and James was real. A reality she couldn't begin to understand.

The following morning, James entered the office at Tandy Stables and found Lily Mae Prescott at her desk, paging through a ledger.

His boss was a tiny-boned woman with sun-baked skin, gray-streaked hair and a tough-as-tar voice. She was also the most disorganized person he'd ever met.

She peered up at him through the silver specs that routinely fell to the end of her nose. "Are you taking a break?"

"If you don't mind." He'd started his shift earlier than usual, helping the ranch hands complete the much-needed repairs at the barn.

"Of course I don't mind. You work your ass off around here."

He couldn't help but smile. She'd commented on his ass before, insisting she'd hired him because she liked the way his butt looked in a pair of jeans. He suspected she'd hired him because she was desperate to fill the job. Her rental stables catered to the tourist trade and her busiest season was about to begin. Plain and simple, she needed an assistant, someone to manage the way she mismanaged the place.

"Mind if I use the computer?" he asked.

She waved her arm. "Go right ahead. You know I hate that fandangle contraption."

Yeah, she hated it all right. She couldn't seem to get the hang of keeping computer records, leaving a drudge of old-fashioned paperwork for him to sort through.

He took a seat at the other desk, and she made an unladylike snort and adjusted her glasses. "I only bought that machine because Harvey Osborn told me to get with the times. Learn to use a computer, he said. Get a Web site. Advertise on the Internet."

James wanted to grin, but he knew she'd get ticked if she knew he was amused. She mentioned Harvey at least once a day.

She made another disgusted sound. "I should have never listened to that old coot."

This time James did grin. When she sent him a sour look, he shrugged and got online.

Then he spent the next ten minutes scanning a melanoma site, reading about the disease, trying to understand what was happening to Emily.

Lily Mae rose to pour herself a cup of coffee and took the liberty of peering over his shoulder. "What are you doing, James?"

"Research."

"Is that what it's called when a man obsesses over a woman?"

He frowned at the monitor. "I'm not obsessing."

"Bull. You can't get that little waitress off your mind."

Frustrated, he turned in his chair. He'd been up half the night, thinking about Emily, recalling his past, the loss of his wife, the horror of the disease that had claimed her. "I want to help Emily, but she won't let me."

"Maybe you're offering the wrong kind of help. Maybe she's tired of worrying about her surgery. Maybe she needs a night on the town."

Suddenly James felt like a big, stupid male. A guy who didn't have enough sense to know what a woman needed. "I should ask her on a date?"

"Afraid she'll turn you down?"

At this point, he honestly didn't know. Emily had acted odd last night. But their whole relationship was odd. "Maybe. But I suppose my ego could take it."

Yet as the day wore on, his ego took a beating. He felt like a dorky teenager stressing about asking the girl he liked to the prom. Finally, he got the guts to call Emily at the diner and ask if she could stop by the stables after she got off work, explaining that there was something he wanted to discuss with her. She sounded wary, but agreed to see him.

She arrived at 4:20, wearing her uniform and a cautious expression. He'd suggested meeting at his living quarters, which was located a short distance from the barn.

He invited her inside, and she stood with her arms crossed, watching him through those emerald eyes.

He dusted his hands on his jeans. Ranch work was dirty, and he knew he looked like a ruffian with his frayed denims and old, washed-too-many-times shirt. In his high-flying mob days, he would have used the damn thing as a rag. In the year and a half he'd spent on the run, the condition of his clothes had been the least of his worries.

"Do you want a soda or something?" he asked.

She shook her head. "No, thank you."

"Mind if I have one?" His mouth had gone dry and wetting his lips wasn't helping.

"Sure, go ahead."

He offered her a seat in his living room and grabbed a can of root beer from the kitchen, then drank half of it in one thirst-quenching swallow.

When he returned, she was perched on the edge of an oak-framed sofa. She looked out of place amid the rugged ranch-style furnishings, but he'd already formed a fairy tale, she-lives-in-a-cottage type impression of her.

"What's going on?" she asked.

He took another swig of the root beer, then placed it on a nearby table. He hated asking women out, hated setting himself up for rejection. "Lily Mae thinks I should take you on a date."

Emily tilted her head. "Why?"

"Because she thinks you need a night on the town."

"I don't want to go on a pity date, James."

"Is that what you think this is?" He dragged a hand across his jaw, felt the rasp of his beard stubble, the ache of wanting to hold her, of needing to protect her. "Lily Mae doesn't pity you and neither do I."

"Don't you?"

"No." It wasn't pity, he thought. It was a hunger that made him crazy, a desperation that hurt the inside of his heart.

She met his gaze, lifted her chin. "All you see when you look at me is a woman with cancer."

He cursed under his breath, something he'd been doing a lot lately. "I see a beautiful woman, Emily. A woman I'm attracted to." A woman who kept him awake at night, who tortured his emotions.

"Right." Her voice took on a sarcastic edge. "First

it was my virginity and now it's the melanoma. You've got so many excuses. So many reasons not to be with me.''

He frowned, jammed his hands into his pockets. ''I'm trying to be a gentleman. Doing my damnedest not to take advantage of you.''

''That's exactly my point. And don't you dare tell me I'm not ready for a lover. I'm old enough to know what I want.''

James didn't know what to say, how to respond, so he finished the soda, his blood going warm. He wanted her. Heaven help him, he did. But he'd been tempering the heat, the sexual urges that made him a man. ''What am I supposed to do? Just have my way with you?''

''Yes. I mean, no.'' She sighed, dreamy, dovelike. ''I want my first time to be gentle. I want to close my eyes when my lover touches me, when he takes me in his arms.''

Her eyelids fluttered, and he went hard, unbelievably hard. He moved closer, and she opened her eyes. As always, they stared at each other, trapped in one of those strangely sexual, strangely awkward moments.

Finally, he sat next to her, and she fidgeted with her purse, as though she suddenly realized what she'd done, how intensely she'd aroused him.

''I have to leave in about twenty minutes,'' she said. ''I have to meet my brother at the bus.''

He searched her gaze. ''Can you arrange for a baby-sitter?''

She blinked, drew a breath. ''For when?''

"Tonight. I want to take you on that date and I want—" He paused, yearning to touch her, to make her fantasy, and his, come alive. He imagined unbuttoning her practical pink uniform and carrying her straight to his rumpled, I'm-so-damn-lonely bed. "And I want you to stay with me after the date. To sleep here."

She pressed her hand to the front of her dress, and he suspected her heart was pounding as rapidly as his. "I'll have to ask Steven's parents if they can keep Corey overnight." She looked away, then back again. "Are you sure, James?"

"Yes." He brushed a stray lock of hair from her cheek. He'd wanted her from the instant, the very second he'd seen her. "I'm sure."

Her voice went quiet, as soft as a whisper. "You're not worried about taking advantage of me anymore?"

"No." He hadn't forgotten about her cancer, but now he understood that she needed intimacy, the kind of intimacy only he could give her. "I'll be good to you. I'll be gentle."

She put her head on his shoulder, and he simply held her. Soon he would be her lover, her first lover, the man she'd been waiting for.

Emily stood in front of a full-length mirror in her bedroom. She'd changed her clothes three times, tossing the rejected outfits onto the back of a chair.

"I think you look great." This came from Diane Kerr, her best friend, the loyal brunette who'd been her partner in girlish giggles and movie-star crushes since sixth grade. Naturally, she'd told Diane about

James, admitting that she was going to sleep with him tonight.

Anxious, she turned to face her friend. The other woman sat on the edge of the bed, her tummy protruding like an overinflated basketball. Diane was seven months pregnant and glowing like the highest wattage of a three-way bulb. She'd married her college sweetheart and lived in an attractive home near the river.

"Are you sure this isn't too tight?" Emily tugged at the body-hugging, gold-toned top.

"Men like tight. I can't wait until I can squeeze back into something like that."

"What about the pants? Are they okay?"

"You can't go wrong with a classic beige trouser. Besides you have a matching jacket. It'll look like a sexy suit."

Emily blew the hair out of her eyes. She'd pinned it up, then had taken it down and scrunched it with a mild hairspray. "I'm so nervous."

Diane handed her the shoes of choice, a pair of three-inch heels. "Just relax and enjoy yourself. He's taking you to dinner, isn't he? You love going out to eat."

"I can't concentrate on food right now." She battled with the straps on her shoes. "All I can think about is what we're going to do after we go back to his place. You should see him. I can't believe I'm lusting after a man with a tattoo and a pierced nipple. Me. Little Emmy Chapman."

"It is wild." Diane paused, then made a concerned

face. "Are you sure you know enough about him to be doing this?"

Did she? No, she thought. Not really. James never talked about himself, never volunteered personal information. "I'm going to get to know him."

"I'll say." Diane glanced at Emily's overnight bag, a leather satchel packed with toiletries and a change of clothes. "This is the most daring thing you've ever done."

"I need him, Di."

"I know. But I wish you'd let me stay and meet him."

"Another time, okay? I don't want him to think I invited my friend over to check him out."

"I suppose that would seem rather high schoolish of you." The mother-to-be rose from the edge of the bed. "I guess I better get going before he shows up." She stopped to cradle her tummy. "What time is he bringing you home tomorrow?"

"About six-thirty. We both have to work."

"Is Steven's mom driving Corey to school?"

"Yes." Steven's family had come to her rescue, agreeing to take Corey for the night, as well as shuffle him off to school the next day.

Emily walked Diane to the door and stepped outside with her. "Call me after work tomorrow," the other woman said.

"I will."

"I want details." Diane waggled her eyebrows. "Hot, torrid details."

Emily laughed and hugged her friend. "The sex diaries of little Emmy Chapman?"

"Exactly." Diane got behind the wheel of her yellow compact, squeezing Emily's hand before she left, giving her one last boost of encouragement. "Have fun tonight."

"I'm certainly going to try."

But as she returned to the house to wait for James, to bring her overnight bag into the living room, her nerves started up again. She pressed a hand to her stomach, trying to ease the jittery tension. She wanted to skip dinner, but she couldn't very well say that to James.

He arrived ten minutes later, looking tall and dark and thrillingly dangerous. Dressed entirely in black, his hair was combed away from his face, exposing rugged angles and bronzed skin.

He handed her a long-stemmed rose, a flower with white and red petals. "The lady at the florist said they're called fire and ice." He stood in the entryway, gazing into her eyes. "The color intrigued me. And so did the name."

She inhaled the rose. The scent was light and sweet. "Thank you, James." This was the second time he'd brought her flowers, but this time, the gesture seemed romantic.

She wanted to kiss him, to slip her arms around his neck and bring her mouth to hers, but she couldn't quite summon the courage to be that bold.

Not now. Not while her nerves were hopping.

"Are you all packed?" he asked. "Do you have everything you need?"

She nodded and gestured to her leather satchel, which she'd stuffed to the gills.

He reached for the bag. "I'm glad you're staying with me tonight, Emily."

Her heart skipped a flip-floppy beat. "Me, too."

After a moment of silence, he said, "Are you hungry?"

"Yes," she lied, wishing the tightness in her stomach would go away.

"Good. So am I." He ushered her out the door and escorted her to his truck.

Emily released an anxious breath. Their dinner date, and the anticipated sex that would soon follow, was about to begin.

Five

James didn't think the date was going well. He'd made reservations at the nicest restaurant in town, but in spite of the candlelit ambience and the secluded location of their booth, he and Emily weren't communicating.

She toyed with her meal, nibbling on tiny bites of steak, stirring the sour cream on her baked potato.

"Is something wrong with your food?" he asked.

She looked up from her plate. "No. It's good. Is your meal all right?"

He nodded. "It's fine." He'd eaten half of his steak and a large portion of his side dishes, which was at least twice as much as she'd consumed. He reached for his beer and took a swig. He suspected she was nervous about their sexual arrangement. Hell, he was nervous, too. Worried about pleasing her, about making her first time special. "Did I tell you how pretty you look?"

She sent him a self-conscious smile, then tugged on her top. The stretchy gold fabric clung to her curves, showcasing the shape of her breasts. "I didn't know what to wear. I changed three times."

He wanted to move to the other side of the booth, to touch her, to ease both of their fears, but he gestured to his shirt instead. "I went out and bought some new duds. So I fussed a little, too."

Her eyes lit up. "You bought new clothes for me?"

He smiled, shrugged a little. "I didn't want to take you out looking like a bum."

"You look incredible, James. But you always do."

"You think?" Giving in to the need to touch her, to get closer, he left his seat.

"What are you doing?" she asked as he scooted in beside her.

"Sitting next to you."

She laughed. "There's not enough room for both of us."

"We'll make do." The cozy, two-person booth was definitely cramped from this side, but her laughter was worth it. "I think I'll sample your meal." He reached for his plate. "And give you some of mine."

She angled her body, pressing her back against the wall so she could face him. Their knees bumped under the table. "You won't like my steak."

"Why not?"

"Because it's well done, and yours is rare."

"I'll survive." As long as she kept looking at him the way she was looking at him now. With stars in her eyes, he thought. With bright, girlish wonder. He picked up his utensils and cut into her steak. Then he chewed, swallowed and washed the too-tough meat down with a swig of beer. "It's not bad. For beef jerky. Now you've got to try mine."

She shook her head. "No way. I don't eat things that haven't quit mooing."

He couldn't help but chuckle. "Come on, take a chance. Do something wild."

"Something wild?" She leaned in close, batted her lashes like a delicious little diva. "You do realize I'm a rare-steak virgin, don't you?"

Thoroughly charmed, he pushed his plate toward her, baiting her with the bloodred meat. "Are you sure you won't let me deflower you?"

"Oh, my."

She fanned her face, feigning a good dose of shock. Then they looked at each other and laughed, enjoying the sexual innuendoes, the silly flirtation, the playful sense of humor they seemed to share.

A moment later, she blindsided him with a serious question. "Why did you move here?"

"What?"

"Why did you move to Silver Wolf?" She dipped into her potato and extended her fork to him. "What made you choose a small town in Idaho?"

He accepted the food she offered, giving himself time to form an answer, to spout a prearranged lie, to convince his conscience that the story WITSEC had created held a semblance of truth.

"I'm a bit of a drifter," he said. "I was restless

and needed a change. A friend of mine suggested this area.''

''The man who was with you when you first came to town?''

Guilty, he took another bite of Emily's potato and offered her a piece of shrimp from his plate. ''Yes.'' Apparently someone had told her that he'd arrived in Silver Wolf with another man. ''His name is Zack.'' Zack Ryder, he thought, conjuring an image of the deputy marshal assigned to his case. ''He's the only person I know in Idaho. But he lives in the city.''

''Have you known him a long time?''

James reached for his beer, tried to act casual. ''Long enough.''

''Where'd you meet him?''

''At an Indian gathering.'' That was a blatant lie, but WITSEC had chosen Ryder as his inspector because they were both mixed bloods. James supposed he and Ryder looked natural together. For a cop and a criminal, he thought. For two men who, aside from the Native blood flowing through their veins, didn't have a damn thing in common.

Emily sipped her water. ''Diane Kerr is my oldest and dearest friend. We see each other all the time.''

Grateful she'd turned the conversation around, offering information about herself, he managed a smile. ''Diane's a lucky girl.''

She smiled, too. ''So am I. I don't know what I'd do without her.''

''It's good to have friends,'' he said as a stab of loneliness pierced his chest.

''Yes, it is.'' She tasted his rice, then went back to

her own meal. "I'm glad we're getting to know each other, James."

When he looked into her eyes, regret washed over him, seeping into his pores, burning his soul. He hated the way the lies made him feel, hated pretending that he was a decent man, someone worthy of her affection, of her trust. He shouldn't have asked her to be with him, but it was too late. He needed her too badly, wanted her too much to let her go.

And she needed him, too. For now, she needed him.

"Should we get dessert later?" she asked.

He blinked, caught the glow in her eyes, the spark of candlelight. "Do you want to?"

"If you do." She motioned to their waiter who was wheeling an array of cakes, custards and chocolate éclairs to another table. "They have a pastry cart."

James studied Emily's eager expression. For a girl who'd been too nervous to eat earlier, she was certainly holding her own.

"Sure," he said. "We can share a couple of desserts. What's your favorite?"

"Everything." She pressed against him to get a better look at the cart as it passed. "All of it. I can never decide."

Such innocence, he thought, as he watched her. Innocence he would steal.

He didn't deserve her, that much he knew. But tonight it didn't matter. He wouldn't feel guilty. He wouldn't let his past destroy this moment, this memory, the knowledge that she was his.

If only for a little while.

* * *

James unlocked his door, and Emily entered his house, carrying a pastry box. They'd shared two decadently rich desserts at the restaurant, but he'd insisted on buying an assortment of treats to take home, which included almost every cream-filled, chocolate-laced, caramel-flavored indulgence they hadn't tried.

He flipped on a light, and she clutched the box to her chest. Suddenly she was nervous again. "Should I put this in the fridge?"

"Sure, go ahead, and I'll take your bag to my room." He indicated the leather satchel slung over his shoulder. "Then you can unpack if you want to."

"Okay." She went to the kitchen and refrigerated the pastries, stood for a moment, took a deep breath and headed for the bedroom.

His bedroom. James Dalton. Her soon-to-be lover.

The hallway was narrow, but the single-wide trailer offered a cozy sort of comfort, with rustic furniture and tan carpeting.

She found James seated on the edge of a queen-size bed, removing his boots. Her bag was next to him.

He looked up and smiled. "I'm just getting comfortable."

Should she take off her shoes, too? When he stood, removed his belt and untucked his shirt, her heartbeat went crazy.

"There's an empty drawer in the dresser," he told her. "I don't use them all."

Normally Emily wouldn't unpack for one night, but she liked the notion of settling in. Somehow it made what was about to happen seem as though she were on her honeymoon. A forbidden honeymoon with a man she was still getting to know, but at least the task helped calm her nerves. She placed her belongings in the drawer, folding them just so. She could feel James behind her, waiting, watching.

''That's pretty,'' he said.

She glanced at the silky nightgown she was about to put away, then she turned in his direction. ''This?''

''Yes.''

''I brought it to sleep in.''

''Wear it now. Wear it for me.''

Her knees went weak; her pulse jumped. At some point, he'd unbuttoned his shirt, and the opened garment gave her an unobstructed view of his navel and the line of hair that disappeared into the waistband of his pants.

''May I use your bathroom?'' She couldn't possibly change in front of him, not now, not like this.

He pointed to the door behind her. ''There's an entrance from here and the hall. That makes it seem more like a master bath, I guess. But you'll have to remember to close both doors when you're in there.'' He shoved his hands in his pockets. ''I'll try to remember, too.''

She reached for the small bag that contained her toiletries. ''It's only for one night.'' And she wouldn't forget to barricade herself in the bathroom, to close both doors and to lock them.

''I hope it turns into more,'' he said.

''More?''

"More than one night. I'd like you to stay here again sometime."

Her stomach fluttered. "Me, too." Did he know how enticing he looked, standing there, gazing at her, with his shirt undone and his hair falling onto his forehead? "I shouldn't be too long."

"I don't mind waiting," he told her.

She gathered her wits and reminded herself to breathe, to allow air to flow in and out of her lungs.

Once she was inside the bathroom, she freshened up and slipped on the emerald-colored nightgown he'd requested, adding a spritz of floral-scented body spray to her neck and shoulders. Unsure of what to do with her other clothes, she left them on top of the hamper in a neatly folded pile.

Giving her hair one last, I-can't-believe-this-is-happening fluff, she stared at her reflection in the mirror. When she summoned the courage to emerge, James still wore his trousers and his shirt was still undone.

"The bathroom is free if you need it," she said, hoping she didn't look as self-conscious as she felt.

"I don't need anything but you." He moved forward, stopped when they were only inches apart. "You're so beautiful. So incredibly beautiful."

"Thank you." She wet her lips, contemplated touching him.

He touched her first, sliding his hands under the straps of her nightgown. "Don't be nervous, Emily."

"I'm not. Not that much," she amended.

"Let me hold you." He took her in his arms, and

she melted against him. For the longest time, they remained, locked in a silent embrace.

When he kissed her, she stood on her toes and welcomed the sensation, the slide of tongue against tongue, body against body. His muscles were taut, the ridge beneath his zipper hard. Greed washed over her, flowing like a river, snaking, swirling, leaving her breathless.

She imagined tearing off his clothes, scraping her nails over all that hot, male skin. "I want to undress you, James."

"We'll undress each other." He eased her onto the bed. "We'll take turns."

She wanted to play first, to fill her senses with her fantasy. She didn't tear off his clothes, but she tugged until his shirt lay on the floor and his pants were undone.

He shifted his weight, and she kissed him, just deep enough to make him groan. He had scars on his chest, healed-over wounds, she suspected, from boyhood skirmishes, from the wildness that came from within.

He reminded her of a panther, of a big, dark cat that didn't know its own strength. When she toyed with the nipple ring, his entire body shuddered.

Fascinated, she sat back to look at him. "It *is* sensitive."

"Extremely. But I like it."

"You're kinky, James Dalton."

He grinned, pounced like the cat he was. Within the blink of an eye, she was beneath him, his lips brushing her ear. "I watched you at the restaurant, Emily, when you were eating your dessert, licking the custard from your spoon." He slid his hands down, along her waist, over her hips. "I want to lick you like that. I want to put my mouth all over you."

She caught her breath, fought a wave of virgin panic. When he looked into her eyes, her cheeks went hot.

He smoothed her hair away from her face. "Has anyone ever done that to you?"

"No." She paused to steady her words, to tell herself there was no reason to feel shy, to panic. "But I've done it. To my high school boyfriend." In a car, she thought, after a football game. "We were parked by the river, making out the way kids do."

James gazed at her mouth, focused on it for a second. "Sweet, innocent Emily." Somehow her admission seemed to arouse him even more. "You never fail to surprise me."

"It was just that once." Just one youthful experience, one teenage curiosity. "And I finished doing it with my hands. I wasn't going to—"

He grinned at her. "Swallow?"

She smacked his shoulder, and they both laughed. "I can't believe I just told you that."

"I'm glad you did." He gave her a tender hug, and they settled into each other's arms. She couldn't have dreamed this moment, dreamed the quiet intimacy, the way her body fit so snugly against his.

She closed her eyes, and he pressed his lips to her ear, rousing her. "Let me show you how good it feels."

Emily opened her eyes, studied him—the way his hair fell across his forehead, the way the light from a nearby lamp sent golden shadows across his face. She couldn't say no.

He peeled off her nightgown and followed the path with his lips, kissing and nibbling along the way. The feeling was unbearable, but she wanted more, as much as he would give her, as much as she could endure.

"James." She breathed his name, and he pulled her panties down, searing her with openmouthed kisses, teasing her with slow, deliberate flicks of his tongue.

She shivered from the swell, from the sensation of saliva to skin. Pleasure poured over her, molten and wet. Anxious, she lifted her hips, tugged at his hair, pulled him closer. So close, she thought she might die.

And when she climaxed, when shock waves slammed through her system, all she could do was clutch the sheets and sink helplessly onto the bed.

James rose to look at Emily, to watch her. Her eyes were closed, her skin was flushed and her hair fell in bewitching disarray.

Intrigued, he moved over her, waited for her to stir.

Finally, she opened her eyes and gazed at him through the aftermath of a deep and drugging orgasm. Sexual delirium, he thought. It looked good on her.

He lowered his head to kiss her, to press his body next to hers. She arched and stretched, bumping her nakedness against his fly. He all but groaned, then struggled to remove his pants, to toss his boxers onto the floor. "Are you ready, Emily?"

She cuddled against him, all warm and soft and sweet, like an unsuspecting kitten. "Yes."

"I don't want to hurt you." But he knew he would. Damn it, he knew he would. "It usually hurts the first time."

"I know, but it doesn't matter."

"Yes, it does." He wanted to give her the fairy tale she deserved. But he didn't know how, so he simply ran his hands over her body, gliding his fingers over her skin. She looked so fair next to him, so fragile.

"Do you want me, James?"

"More than anything."

"Then take me." She reared up to kiss him, to nibble coyly on his lips, to stroke between his legs. "Take what you want."

He lost it. Totally lost it. The hunger inside him exploded, and he pushed his tongue into her mouth and rolled her across the bed, tangling the sheets.

Her hands quested, and he relished the heat, the pressure of her fingers, the incredible feeling of being in a woman's arms, of seeing desire in her eyes.

It made him seem whole, real, decent. So for now, he chose to believe the lie, to let himself fall into the fantasy of being Emily's lover.

He released a ragged breath, straddled her, watched as she waited. The condoms were in his nightstand, and the nightstand was within arm's reach. He grabbed what he needed, fumbled with the foil and cursed his clumsiness.

Finally, finally, he rolled on the protection, felt her shift beneath him, open her thighs, welcome his penetration.

Then she tensed, and he knew he'd caused her pain. "I'm sorry," he said.

"Just don't stop."

"I won't." He couldn't, he thought. Being inside her felt too good. Too right. She clamped around him like a velvet vise, and he pushed deeper.

She tensed again, bit down on her bottom lip. He kept moving, slowly, gently, promising in soothing whispers it wouldn't hurt next time.

Then something changed. Her gazed locked on to his, and he suspected her pain was subsiding. She pressed against him, crushing her breasts to his chest, flattening the nipple ring, sending a shiver straight up his spine.

He groaned, and she smiled, as tempting as a green-eyed nymph. "I think I'm starting to like this."

"Oh, yeah?" His heart leaped to his throat. She was warm and wet and incredibly tight. He sure as hell liked it.

She began to move beneath him, to test the rhythm he'd set, to meet his strokes with dream-induced glory. They could have been dancing, he thought. Moving to a song only they could hear.

He wanted her to climax again, so he slid his hand between their bodies and rubbed that sensitive little spot that made women crazy.

It made him crazy, too. Erotic insanity. He couldn't get enough.

James sought her mouth, losing himself in the passion, in the thrill, in the surrender of a woman who gave him everything he'd been missing.

Everything he wished he could keep.

Six

Emily awakened during the predawn hour. The hour the sky prepared for the sun. The hour a hazy glow bled through the blinds, washing the room in muted colors and dancing shadows.

She'd slept spoon-style with James all night, the back of her body tucked cozily against the front of his. She could feel him breathing into her hair. Rough breaths, a little raspy.

She suspected he used to smoke. Strange, the things she was learning about him. But Emily was learning about herself, too. Being naked with a man first thing in the morning was strangely compelling, an unfamiliar occurrence she could certainly get used to.

He mumbled and shifted, pulling her closer, burying his face deeper into her hair. She knew he liked her honey-colored hair. He'd mentioned it on the day they'd met.

"Are you awake?" she asked.

"No."

She smiled into her pillow. "You sound awake."

"Then I'm half-awake. How'd you sleep?"

"Like a dream." Emily turned in his arms. She wanted to look at him, to see the man she'd made love with. Curious, she met his unfocused gaze and saw him squint into the dim light. A hint of beard stubble peppered his jaw, and his hair was flat in some areas and sticking up in others. He couldn't have been more gorgeous. Rough around the edges worked on James. It was part of who he was.

"I need to get up," he said. "I've got to pee."

She nearly laughed. She'd never known anyone quite like him. He climbed out of bed and stumbled to the bathroom, forgot to close the door, then remembered a second later.

Had he ever lived with anyone? she wondered.

Yes, she decided. He had. The mystery blonde, the woman Emily reminded him of, must have shared more than just an occasional romp in his bed. James had been in love with her. That much seemed clear, obvious from the beginning.

Troubled, Emily sat up and frowned. Would it be all right to ask him about his former lover? To question him about her? Or would that be a foolish thing to do on their first morning after?

"What's wrong?"

His voice came out of nowhere, giving her a start. She looked up, then realized she was hugging his pillow, cradling it, possessing it. "Nothing's wrong."

"You're frowning."

She tried to change her expression, to appear unaffected by her thoughts. "I'm fine. Should we get up or go back to sleep?"

He glanced at the clock, then moved toward her, tall and dark and naked. Her heart did a girlish flop.

"Let's stay in bed." He crawled in beside her and resumed the position they'd slept in, pulling her tight against him, bumping his pelvis against her rear.

"Mmm." She melted; she simply melted. Nothing, absolutely nothing, had ever felt this good, this right, this secure. She snuggled into the feeling, wiggling her bottom.

He made a tortured sound. "You're cheating, Emily."

"What? Oh." She smiled, suddenly aware of what she'd done. "Sorry."

"Don't apologize." He nuzzled the side of her neck and cupped her breasts, rubbing his thumbs over her nipples. Pleasure, sweet and thick, glided through her. She attempted to turn, to face him, but he stopped her.

"Stay there, baby. Just like that."

"James?"

"Shhh." One of his hands slid between her thighs. He caressed her, lightly, steadily, stoking a fire, building pressure, promising relief.

She went damp, slick and moist against his hand. He whispered something in her ear, something erotic, something forbidden.

She gasped, moaned, nearly climaxed on the spot.

Her eyes turned glassy, her mind fogged. She couldn't see straight, couldn't think clearly. All she wanted was to kiss him, to suck mercilessly on his tongue. But she couldn't. His mouth was already busy, biting the back of her neck. Like a stallion, she thought, preparing to mount a mare.

She hadn't considered making love in this position, but she could feel him, hard and heavy, fully aroused, eager to stake his claim. He took her hand and encouraged her to touch herself, to rub the wetness, to spread the moisture while he sheathed himself with a condom.

Then he grasped her hips, angled her body to accommodate him and plunged deep. She twisted to kiss him, and their mouths mated, the flavor as heady, as hot, as carnal as the sex.

Tongues clashed, teeth scraped, hormones surged to undeniable peaks.

Emily went mad. She ached to take more of him, to let him invade her very soul. She wanted him forever, just like this, pushing her to the edge of sanity, holding her there.

He licked the shell of her ear, nibbled her lobe, said something naughty again.

An orgasm exploded behind her eyes, bursting in a flash of color. Silver, gold, red. She held fast to the arms snaked around her waist, held fast to the man fueling her deepest, darkest fantasies.

He made a rough, primal sound, and she knew he was spilling his seed, releasing the pressure in his loins. She twisted to kiss him again and he devoured her in one earth-shattering taste.

When it ended, when they could draw breath, his sweat-slicked body fell against hers, pinning her to the bed. Finally, she moaned, and he mumbled and moved, freeing her from his weight.

''Sorry.''

"Don't be." She reached for a rumpled corner of the sheet, felt it slide through her fingers. "We should do that again."

"Right now?" he asked.

"Right this second," she responded, before they found the energy to laugh. They could barely lift their heads.

Eventually James summoned the strength to rise, to walk to the bathroom, to dispose of the condom, she assumed. When he returned and tried to settle back into bed, the alarm clock went off. He cursed and smacked the button, silencing the sound.

"I can't believe it's time to get up."

She turned to look at him, to check out that long, muscular body. She glanced down, saw that he was still partially aroused. "You've already been up."

He tapped her nose and made it twitch. "Funny girl."

Bad boy, she thought, recalling the hot-and-nasty things he'd whispered in her ear.

"Do you want breakfast?" he asked.

She wasn't quite ready to switch gears, to leave the cozy comfort of his bed, even if it was time to get her lazy butt moving. She searched for her nightgown, deciding the least she could do was get dressed. "Are you fixing it?"

He grabbed a pair of boxers from his drawer and shrugged into them. "As in cooking? At this time of the morning? I was thinking more along the lines of a cup of coffee and a cream puff. Or a Napoleon or whatever the hell those things we brought home last night are called."

She couldn't help but laugh. "That sounds like a fine breakfast, James."

"You bet it does. Nothing gets a body going like caffeine and sugar."

Within no time, he'd brewed a pot of coffee and they sat in the middle of his bed and made pigs of themselves. Emily couldn't remember the last time she'd had so much fun. Or felt so alive.

Today she wasn't a cancer patient. She was simply a woman. James Dalton's woman.

"When can I see you again?" he asked.

She licked chocolate from her fingers and imagined kissing him sweet and senseless. "Whenever you want."

"I'm going to hold you to that."

"You better," she told him, wondering if this moment—or this man—could get any better.

On Sunday morning, Emily battled with her brother. She glanced at James, but he stood by quietly, staying out of the way. He'd invited Corey to Tandy Stables, offering to bring the boy to work with him, to let him play cowboy for a day. But their outing had yet to begin and already Corey was acting up. Exhausted, Emily blew a frustrated breath. The kitchen had become a war zone.

"I don't like it," Corey complained. "It smells funny."

"It does not." She tried to rub sunscreen onto his skin, but he jerked back, refusing to let her touch his face. "If you don't wear this, you're staying home."

"It's not like I'm going swimming."

"It doesn't matter. You're still going to be in the sun all day."

"This is stupid." Corey scrunched his nose, then plopped himself down at the table. Emily knew she couldn't pass herself off as Corey's mother, and he knew it, too. A nagging sibling didn't earn the same respect as a nagging parent.

"It's not stupid." James moved forward. "Too much sun can hurt people. It can make them sick."

"Not me," the child insisted.

"Emily has to have surgery, Corey. The sun made her sick. And you're her brother. You have the same genes."

The boy glanced at his Levi's. "I'm not wearing Emmy's jeans."

James managed a smile. "I was talking about a different kind of genes. Your skin is light, like hers. And the lotion she wants you to wear will protect you."

Emily studied her lover, listened to the sincerity in his voice. Two days had passed since she'd spent the night at his house. Two days of stealing quick, choppy kisses, of battling work schedules that didn't mesh, of dodging her little brother's curious glances.

Emily could have just told Corey that she was dating James, but she wasn't ready to make that kind of commitment. Nor was she ready to sleep with someone she wasn't married to, at least not in front of her brother.

"Girls wear that stuff." Corey wasn't buying it, not even from his newfound idol, the man he openly admired. "It even smells girly."

James took the bottle from Emily and sniffed it.

She watched him, her heart going uncomfortably soft. He hadn't mentioned her cancer since they'd made love, but it was still there, floating between them. And today it had risen to the surface.

"Smells okay to me," James said.

"Then you wear it," came the youthful reply.

"Fine. I will." James proceeded to put the sunscreen on his face and arms, rolling his sleeves up even farther. He wore a rugged ensemble of denim and leather, with a cowboy hat shading his eyes.

Those eyes, Emily thought. Those haunted eyes. Sometimes when he looked at her, she wondered what he was thinking, what he was feeling.

Corey squared his narrow shoulders, attempting, it appeared, to maintain his boys-don't-wear-lotion dignity. "Just give me the dumb stuff." He shot Emily a warning glance. "But I'm putting it on myself."

The six-year-old smeared the dreaded sunscreen all over his face and arms, using far too much and rubbing the excess on his pants. He needed a man around, Emily thought. He needed the kind of influence only his gender could provide.

"Go put your boots on," she told him. "You can't go to Tandy Stables without your boots."

Corey left his chair. "My hands are all yucky now."

"Then wash them."

He huffed out a breath. "This is such a hassle."

"I know." Trapped in emotion, Emily went to her brother. She would never forget the day her parents had died, the day Corey had been orphaned. "But it's something we can't change." She knelt to lift his chin, to look into his eyes. "I have to be careful in the sun, and so do you."

"And James, too?"

"Yes," she said. "And James, too." Although she knew he wasn't at risk for melanoma, not the way she and Corey were.

The crisis ended and Corey decided his hands weren't that yucky after all, but he still needed to put on his boots. He tore off down the hall, leaving the adults alone.

After a moment of silence, James reached for the sunscreen and capped the bottle. "Corey is confused."

"I know." Emily scanned the kitchen. This wasn't the house she'd grown up in. She'd sold the other one, unable to cope with the memories, with vestiges from the past. "He doesn't understand. Not completely."

James moved closer. "You seem confused, too."

"I'm fine. Just emotional, I guess."

"Your surgery is only five days away."

She twisted a strand of her hair, wished this conversation wasn't so awkward. Nonetheless she had to ask, "Are you going to be there?"

He searched her gaze. "Do you want me to be there?"

Yes, she thought, cursing her vulnerability. She wanted him to drive her to the hospital, to stay nearby, to keep her safe. "It shouldn't matter. I shouldn't need you."

"We need each other, Emily."

"Do we?" She glanced at the counter, felt her

pulse race, locked her fingers to keep her hands from quaking. "For more than just sex?"

He had the audacity to smile. "I don't know. We've only done it that one time."

"We've done it twice," she corrected before she punched his arm and made him laugh. Good God, he could be annoying. If he wasn't torturing her with those troubled eyes, he was cracking silly jokes. "I was going to let you sneak into my room tonight, but—"

"But what?"

"I changed my mind."

"Wanna bet?" Quick and carnal, he dragged her against his body and kissed her, making her heart spin like a valentine-shaped top.

She invited him to her bed.

A quarter moon shimmered in the sky and leaves on trees rustled in the breeze. James cut across Emily's yard and released the air in his lungs. Tonight, he wasn't dressed like a cowboy. He'd chosen a dark pullover, black pants and soft-soled shoes. Clothes he'd worn a dozen times before.

He made it to her window and stood in the shadows. A cricket chirped, but he ignored the sound. He was used to nocturnal creatures; he was one of them.

He arched his body, closed his eyes, felt that cat-burglar rush of adrenaline.

Rush of excitement? James opened his eyes and cursed beneath his breath. What in the hell was he doing?

Breaking and entering, his conscience said. Like the low-down, scum-sucking thief he was. He dragged his hand through his hair and cursed again, his language fouler this time.

There was nothing to steal in Emily's bedroom.

Nothing but her heart.

He shook his head, chasing away the thought. Was he crazy? Losing the last of his sanity? He had no business trying to steal her heart. James Dalton wasn't real. He was an illusion, a sleight of hand, a trick of the mind. If Emily fell for him, she would be falling for the man the government had created, not the man behind the mask.

So get the hell out of here. Abandon this insane notion of slipping into her room, of climbing into her bed.

But it was her idea, he reminded himself. He wasn't breaking and entering. She'd promised to leave her window unlocked for him.

Then why did he feel like he was about to commit a crime? He inched closer to the window. Because he knew he could invade Emily's house without an invitation. He had years of experience, years of breaking into people's homes and taking what he wanted.

Jewels, cash, priceless objects.

But this was different. There were no alarm systems to dismantle, no security cameras to dodge, no guard dogs to foil, nothing challenging his path.

Just an unlocked window. Child's play.

Only he wasn't a child. He was a grown man, anxious to be near a woman, to touch her, to put his hands all over her naked body.

Violent hands, he thought. Fingerprints that were on file. James knew what he was. He used to pound his fists into other men's faces, pick bar fights just so he could taste his own blood. His IQ made him cocky, and being a soldier in the mob had made him an accessory to murder.

And now here he was, pretending to be someone else.

What choice did he have? he asked himself. Without WITSEC he would be hiding from the mob on his own. Or lying face first in a shallow ditch somewhere, a well-aimed bullet in his back.

As if any of that mattered. He didn't have anything to live for. His wife was dead, and he would never see his sister or his son again. By now, his baby boy wouldn't even remember him. There was no one. Nothing.

Except Emily.

With his heart pounding in his throat, he tried the window, opened it, slipped inside like the pro he was.

The room was dark except for the flicker of two scented candles. Strawberry smoke and the anticipation of sex. His head swam with it.

He stood in the corner, a tall, quiet shadow in the dark. He knew Emily hadn't heard him come in. He could see her, curled up on her bed, glancing at the clock on her nightstand, waiting for him to arrive.

But James was early. The element of surprise. It thrilled him, shamed him, made him want her even more.

A warrior in his prime, he dashed across the room, seized her shoulders and kissed her before she could scream. She gasped into his mouth. He took her tongue and made her moan.

When she was wide-eyed and breathless, he released her. He'd never been so damned aroused.

"James. Oh, my God, James. How did you do that?"

Blood surged to his loins. Her nightie was the size of a floral-printed postage stamp. "You left the window unlocked."

"But I didn't even know you were here. And then you..." Her words trailed. "You..."

"I kissed you. I've done it before."

"Not like that." She sighed; she literally sighed. "That was magic."

No, he thought. That was the work of a professional thief. He reached for the ribbon on her nightgown. She'd tied it in a pretty little bow. He tugged at it, loosened it, destroyed the bow.

She watched him, candlelight flickering in her eyes. He lifted the thigh-length garment, found her naked underneath. "No panties?"

"I must have forgot."

He smiled and pushed her onto the bed. Then they went insane, crazier than he could have imagined. He ripped her nightie in two; she yanked at his fly and broke the zipper. He kicked off his shoes; she pulled his shirt over his head and tugged at his nipple ring.

James bit back the pain, the pleasure, the groan buried deep in his chest. They couldn't make orgasmic noises. They couldn't wake her brother.

Emily lowered her head to his lap. He was certain he was going to die. She took him into her mouth, took him so deep, he fisted her hair and prayed for relief.

She was lethal, he thought, as his mind blurred. Sweet and soft and innocently lethal.

And if she didn't stop...

He dragged her up, shoved her back down, let her suck him again. But this time she lifted her head on her own and kissed his navel, licking her way to his nipple.

"You should pierce the other one," she said.

"And the things you do to a man should be outlawed."

She dropped her hand, closed her fingers around him. "I have some experience in this area."

"Remind me to thank your high school boyfriend." He took her in his arms, held tight. "After I beat the crap out of him."

She smiled. "You're jealous?"

"Damn straight."

Silence. Another smile. "Did you remember to bring a condom?"

"Always." He held up the foil and it winked like a star. In the next instant, they were kissing, caressing, exchanging fantasies.

Sensation slid over sensation, like silk over skin. When he entered her, she lifted her hips, taking him deep, accepting every stroke, every sweet thrust of pleasure. He rode her, warmth flooding his body.

It was like riding a dream.

Beautiful sex. Dangerous sex. Her hands sought his and their fingers entwined. It was the kind of intimacy he missed, the kind that condemned a criminal's soul. He lowered his head to kiss her, to taste her lips, to show her how much he needed her.

But the need was too great, the hunger too strong. The dream ended in a hard, desperate climax, in a rush of heat and tangled limbs.

They separated, their hearts beating madly. She turned to look at him. Sweet, innocent Emily.

She touched the side of his face. "Did your family call you Jimmy when you were young?"

Jimmy? He squeezed his eyes shut. His name was Reed. Reed Blackwood. "No. I've always been James."

"James fits you. Like James Dean. Now there was a sexy guy." She arched like a sleek, little cat. "Jimmy works, too. Jimmy Dean." She paused, stifled a giggle, lost it and laughed. "That's the name of the sausage guy, isn't it?"

He laughed, too. She made it easy to forget about Reed Blackwood. "This isn't exactly the most appropriate time to discuss sausages."

"Really?" She leaned on her elbow. "Why not?"

He rolled over and tickled her, and she squealed and called him Jimmy.

But as footsteps sounded from outside the room, they both froze. She put her finger over her mouth, signaling a hush. He wasn't about to talk. He suspected her brother was stumbling his way to the bathroom, making an after-midnight pit stop.

They waited for what seemed like forever. Finally a door squeaked and the footsteps disappeared down the hall.

"Close call," she said.

"Yeah." He reached for her, and she snuggled into his embrace. He trailed a finger down her body and stopped at her thigh, but his touch wasn't sexual, and she seemed to sense his concern. "Where is it, Emily?"

"The cancer?" Her voice turned quiet. "It's where your tattoo is."

His breath stilled, but only for a moment. "I should be surprised, but I'm not." James didn't believe in coincidence. To him, that was a fraudulent word for fate. "How long will you be in the hospital?"

"Twenty-three hours. That's how long I can stay and still maintain an outpatient status."

He kept her close, tight against his body. "You know I'm going to be there, don't you?"

"I wasn't sure."

"I wanted to go to the hospital from the beginning."

"I know, but I wasn't comfortable about it then." She turned to look at him. "Now I'm glad you're going to be there."

"Because you need me?"

"Yes." She moved over him, kissed him, made his heart yearn foolishly for hers. "Because I need you."

Seven

James sat in a waiting room at the hospital, staring at the walls, counting the minutes that ticked by.

Emily hadn't told him that the melanoma might have spread to her lymph nodes. He'd assumed the wide local excision surgery would rid her of the cancer, but that might not be the case.

He blew an anxious breath, walked to the vending machines, then chose a bag of peanuts and a carbonated drink. He needed to eat a real meal, he supposed. But this was about all his stomach could handle.

"James?" a feminine voice said from behind him.

He turned around, expecting to see a nurse. Instead he nearly bumped into a pregnant brunette in a yellow dress. He started, took a step back. "Sorry."

"That's okay. You're James. Aren't you?"

"Yes."

"I'm Diane Kerr. Emily's friend."

He took the hand she offered and struggled to get a grip on his emotions. "Emily told me about you." But she hadn't mentioned that Diane was expecting. He glanced at her tummy, figured her to be about six or seven months along. James wasn't an expert, but his wife and his sister had been pregnant during their run from the mob. He'd delivered both babies, experiences he would never want to repeat. His son had been healthy and strong. But his nephew, his sister's tiny infant, had been stillborn.

"Is this your first?" he asked.

She nodded, flashed a mother-in-waiting smile. "According to the ultrasound, it's a boy."

"Congratulations."

"Thank you."

He motioned to the vending machines. "Can I get you anything?"

"Thanks, but I'm fine. I've eaten plenty of junk today." She paused, met his gaze. "How's Emily?"

His heart bumped his chest. "She's in surgery. It's going to be a while."

Diane headed for a chair in the waiting room. "Was she in good spirits?"

"She seemed to be."

"Because you were with her."

He waited until Diane sat, then took a chair. He didn't know how to respond to her comment. His attachment to Emily wasn't something he could discuss. At times, he still felt like an intruder. A lowlife. An ex-con deceiving a community of honest, hardworking people.

He reached for his soda and studied Emily's friend. She had pixie-cut hair, warm brown eyes and girl-next-door dimples. What would she think if she knew the truth about him? Would she be so accommodating? So kind?

"You were going to drive Emily to the hospital," he said. "But I took your place."

"It doesn't matter. Emily needed you to be with her. If it were me, I'd want my husband there."

He glanced away, looked back, took a much-needed breath. "I'm not her husband, Diane."

"Oh, of course not." She waved her hand, making light of a conversation that had gone bone deep. "I didn't mean it like that."

They remained silent for a while. Strangers, he thought, trapped in an uncomfortable situation.

Finally he said, "I wanted to be with Emily. I wanted to be here." Because the bond between them was too strong, because the magic that consumed them couldn't be denied. "But I don't understand why she didn't tell me the cancer might have spread to her lymph nodes."

"Even if it has, it's still treatable."

He thought about Beverly, about how advanced her cancer had been, about how quickly she'd died. "From what I've read, thinner melanomas are less likely to affect the lymph nodes."

"That's true. But Emily is borderline, I think. They just want to be sure. That's why they scheduled a sentinel node biopsy with her surgery."

"I know, but it still worries me."

"The biopsy is important."

James merely nodded. He understood that the surgical team would map the drainage pattern of Emily's lymph nodes, then remove a sentinel node and dissect it. If they discovered cancer, they would remove additional lymph nodes. But if they didn't find any obvious evidence of the disease, further dissection would be done at a lab, where a pathologist would look for a microscopic form of the disease. "I thought her surgery would take care of the cancer. I thought excising the primary tumor would be enough."

"Emily is going to be fine," Diane assured him. "With or without lymph node detection."

James glanced at the clock. "I just hate waiting around like this." And until Emily was home and tucked safely into her bed, he wasn't about to relax.

"I'm fine," Emily said, even though she looked tired, the circles around her eyes a telltale sign.

"You just got home from the hospital." And James wasn't about to let her out of bed, not today.

"You don't have to baby me."

"The hell I don't." He frowned, the tension in his chest working itself into a knot. Her test results wouldn't be available for a week, maybe two. "You should have told me you needed that biopsy. You should have warned me ahead of time."

"I didn't think about it."

"Bull."

She lifted her chin a notch. "Don't get surly."

"Fine, but I'm staying here until you recover." A decision he'd made on the way home from the hospital. "It's easier than stopping by every night after work."

"You can't sleep in my room when Corey's here."

"So I'll sleep on the couch." James scooted onto the bed and sat next to her, mindful of the bandaged scar on her leg. "When Corey gets back from Steven's house, he and I can spend some time together. He'll like that, don't you think?"

"Yes, I'm sure he will."

"And what about you?"

She gave him a smile that tugged at his heart. "I suppose I can put up with having you around." She skimmed his jaw, as though memorizing him with her fingers, with a featherlight touch. "A girl could do worse."

"So could a guy." He released the air in his lungs, felt the knot in his chest loosen. He couldn't handle a rejection, not now. Maybe not ever, but he didn't want to dwell on what the future might bring.

Why? Because it scared him? Because James Dalton would always be Reed Blackwood? And Reed would always be hiding from the mob?

She dropped her hand. "I should call Corey."

"I already did." James tried to clear his mind, to let Reed go. "Steven's dad took the boys out for pizza. They'll be back in an hour or so."

Emily picked up the teddy bear she kept on her nightstand. "That's good. Corey likes pizza." She turned and made the bear cuff him on the nose. "This is Dee-Dee."

He laughed and pulled back to study the toy. Although its faded pink fur was matted, it was still cute.

Sweet and girlish, he supposed. "Have you had Dee-Dee a long time?"

"Since my first day of kindergarten. I bawled like a baby that day. I didn't want to leave my parents." She wiggled the bear's arms, but a moment later, her voice turned sad. "God, I miss them so much."

He looked into her eyes and saw her loss. No matter how much he tried, he couldn't replace her family. "Tell me about them, Emily. Tell me who they were."

She responded quickly, needing, it seemed, to confide in him. "They were from Oregon, but they moved to Idaho after they got married. My mom was a housewife and my dad was an electrician."

"An electrician?" He refrained from admitting that electronics was his passion, that security systems were his specialty. "Was your dad a contractor?"

She shook her head. "He didn't have his own company. He worked for someone else."

And James used to build surveillance equipment in his spare time, a skill he'd lent to the mob. He wasn't anything like Emily's father. He'd barely worked an honest day in his life. "How'd your parents meet?"

"They were high school sweethearts. I always thought that was romantic."

He didn't comment. But how could he? He wasn't an authority on romance. What he knew about love still hurt. "Why did Corey come along so late? Why did they wait so long to have their second child?"

She smiled, even though her eyes had turned misty. "They wanted more children, but it never happened.

So when they were older, they gave up on the idea, and my mom had her tubes tied. Just in case.''

James lifted his brows. ''And that's when she got pregnant?''

''Sometimes tubal ligations fail.'' She propped Dee-Dee on her lap. ''Corey was their miracle baby. That kid was determined to be born.'' When she paused, he could sense her next words, knowing they would ring of death. ''My brother was only three when they passed away.''

''And you were nineteen.''

''Almost twenty.'' She reached for the sheet, then tucked it around the bear, putting it to bed, keeping it safe. ''My parents went to the mountains to cele-brate their anniversary. They owned a little fishing cabin. It was their favorite getaway.'' Her features tightened. ''I stayed home to take care of Corey. They were only supposed to be gone for a few days.''

He didn't ask how they'd died, but he knew she would tell him.

Memories edged her voice, the kind of memories James kept hidden.

''There was a carbon monoxide leak at the cabin. They didn't know about it, of course.'' She took a breath, let it out slowly. ''They fell asleep and never woke up.''

''I'm sorry.''

''Sometimes it's just so hard. I don't have any fam-ily left. My paternal grandparents were already gone, and I've never had any relatives on my mom's side. She was raised in foster care.''

He wished he knew how to comfort her. That he

was strong enough to take away her pain. She closed her eyes, and he touched the ends of her hair. He knew how it felt to grieve, to cry, to pray for the loneliness to end.

As he pressed his lips to her temple, her lashes fluttered. Then her eyes were open and locked on to his. "The people in this town have been good to Corey and me. When it happened, they rallied around us, doing whatever they could. I wouldn't have survived without their support." She kept her gaze on his. "You're like them, James. You belong here."

No, he thought. He didn't. He wanted to fit in, to be part of Silver Wolf, but the lies kept gnawing at his gut. WITSEC should have relocated him to a metropolis, to an overpopulated city. Small-town life was too complicated for a criminal.

And so were his feelings for Emily.

He covered her with the quilt. She still looked tired, vulnerable in a way that made him ache. "You need to rest."

She didn't argue. "Maybe for a little while. Just a nap." He started to rise, but she stopped him. "Don't go. Stay with me until I fall asleep."

"Are you sure? I don't want to disturb you."

"I'm sure." She snuggled against him, and he put his arms around her, needing to keep her close.

Emily awakened the next morning and realized she'd slept through the night. Some nap, she thought, blinking through the haze.

She sat up and looked around, wondering where

James was. She knew he'd taken the weekend off, so he had to be someplace close by.

She went into the bathroom and squinted at the mirror, then washed her face and brushed her teeth, deciding her sleep-ravaged hair could wait. She wanted to see James.

She found him in the kitchen, making a pot of coffee. His back was turned, so she simply watched him. He wore jeans, no shirt and no shoes. When he spilled coffee grounds onto the counter, she smiled.

Then he seemed to sense her presence. He spun around and her heart skipped like a jumping bean.

"Emily? What are you doing out of bed?"

Did he have any idea how gorgeous he looked? Big and tall and tousled in the morning light? "I slept for almost fourteen hours. I think I'm entitled to get out of bed."

"Did you change your bandage?"

"Not yet."

"Do you want me to do it for you?"

She took a step back. "No." She didn't want him fussing over her scar, looking at the ugly wound on her leg. "I can handle it."

He brushed his hands on his jeans. "Does it hurt?"

She shook her head. "It's more tight than painful."

He moved closer. "Sit down and I'll get you a cup of tea."

Confused, she looked past him. "I thought you were making coffee."

"I bought green tea for you. It's supposed to be beneficial for cancer patients."

Emily sighed. She knew he was worried about her

upcoming biopsy results. She was worried, too. But she didn't want him treating her as if she were a walking, talking disease. "I'd prefer coffee."

"Too bad. You're getting tea."

"And you're acting like Nurse Rachett."

Rather than respond, he shot her an exasperated look.

She bit back an amused smile. "Come to think of it, wasn't there an Indian in that movie? A big, strong silent type?"

"Yeah. The guy who busted down the walls. Is that what I'm going to have to do to take care of you?"

Such dedication, she thought. Such tough-guy determination. "Fine, Mr. Sourpuss, I'll try your stupid tea."

"Damn right you will."

In one eye-blinking swoop, he crossed the kitchen and took her in his arms. She caught her breath, then fell willingly into his embrace. "You drive me crazy, James Dalton."

"Emily flew over the cuckoo's nest," he said and made her laugh.

They separated to gaze at each other. And when he skimmed her cheek, she all but melted. His touch was gentle, but his fingers were rough. She liked the sensation.

Was he her guardian angel? she wondered. A wild creature with golden skin and big, dark wings? Half man, she thought. And half crow.

"You're magic," she said.

He didn't respond. Instead, he kissed her. The kind of kiss that slipped into a woman's heart, the kind she dreamed about when she was alone, when she imagined heroes on horseback and castles floating in the sky.

Lost, Emily closed her eyes and took what he offered. And when it ended, she knew she'd been bewitched.

"Let me get your tea," he said as she struggled to steady her pulse.

They sat across from each other at the table, sipping hot drinks and eating toast and jam.

"Being babied isn't so bad," she told him.

"You still look tired."

"Because I overslept."

"Because you're worn-out."

That was true, she supposed. The surgery had taken its toll. "I have plenty of time to recuperate."

"Some vacation."

She went after a second slice of toast. The jam was sweet and thick, laden with strawberries. "It's turning out pretty good so far."

He smiled. But a second later, he frowned at his plate, and she knew his thoughts had drifted to something else. Or to *someone* else.

"Did she hurt you, James?"

He lifted his head. "What?"

"The woman I remind you of? Did she hurt you?"

"No."

"Then why aren't you with her anymore?"

"I'm just not."

"But why?" She searched his gaze and saw the pain he couldn't seem to hide. "It's obvious that you loved her."

He reached for his coffee, took a sip, set it down with unsteady hands. "I don't want to talk about this."

"That's not fair. It's not…" Her words faded and suddenly she knew. She could sense the truth. "She died, didn't she? That's why you're not with her."

He went still, unnaturally still. He could have been made of stone.

Emily's breath hitched. "Answer me."

Silence. Complete silence.

"Damn it, James. Answer me."

"Yes," he snapped. "She's dead."

"From what? Cancer?" When he flinched, she gripped the table. "That's it, isn't it?" The reason he was so determined to baby her, to be with her. "You should have told me."

"I'm sorry, but I couldn't. I just couldn't."

She fought back tears, refusing to cry in front of him. It wasn't her he cared about. It was the other woman who mattered to him, the blonde she represented.

"Don't hate me," he said.

Hate him? She crossed her arms, hugging away the chill. She could never hate him. Not James, not her beautiful, tortured lover. Yet his betrayal lanced her like a dull, dizzying blade. Everything inside her ached—her heart, her soul, the scar on her leg.

Dear God. What was happening to her?

"I'm sorry," he said again.

When the room begun to spin, she rose. "I have to lie down." She lost her footing and started to fall.

And then suddenly he was there, her guardian angel, lifting her into his arms, enfolding her in his wings.

He carried her to bed, and she broke down and cried. He rocked her, holding her as close as possible, and she suspected he was as confused as she was. She could feel his heart slamming against his chest.

She clung to his shoulders, and he whispered another apology, soothing her with his voice, with the sincerity of his sorrow.

Finally, she wiped her tears. He hadn't betrayed her, not purposely. "Do you look at me and see her? Are you mixing us up in your mind?"

"I might have done that in the beginning, but things are different now. I know who you are, and I know that I need you. But what's happening between us scares me."

It scared her, too. He'd become part of her, part of an ache she couldn't deny. What would she do without him?

"Don't hold this against me, Emily."

Afraid she was losing him, she reached for his hand. Her protector, her dark-winged angel. "I won't. And I won't ask you about the woman you loved. But someday you have to tell me about her. Promise me that much."

"I will," he said, before he glanced away and hid the haunting she still saw in his eyes.

Eight

Three days later Emily retreated to her studio. It wasn't much of a studio, she supposed. But the tiny room was laced with art supplies and that counted for something. She enjoyed the creative solace it provided.

Aside from a few art classes in high school, Emily didn't have any formal training. But that hadn't stopped her from selling some of her work.

Maybe James would attend the next craft fair with her. Maybe—

She studied the drawing that occupied her mind. The half-naked, dark-winged image that seduced her imagination was James.

When the door flew open, she closed the sketchbook and spun around in her chair.

Corey bounced in place, bobbing from one foot to

the other. Her brother had returned yesterday. "Are you making pictures, Emmy?"

"Yes." She smiled at his expression, at the boyish enthusiasm he couldn't seem to contain.

"Know what me and James are doin'?"

"No, what?"

"Cooking dinner."

"Really?"

"Yep. And we're all gonna eat on the patio. James bought some candles for the table. He's trying to make it nice for you. He said girls like candles and stuff." He twitched his nose and sent a scatter of freckles dancing. "They're the kind that'll keep the bugs away, too."

Her smile deepened. "Of course. We wouldn't want bugs at our table."

"Girls don't like bugs."

"Certainly not."

"The food is gonna be real good, Emmy. So you gotta come outside in about ten minutes, okay?" He held up his hand. "But not before, 'cause it won't be ready. And I still gotta pick some flowers."

He tore off before she could thank him for being such a gentleman. He banged the door on his way out and made her laugh. Recovering from surgery wasn't so bad, not with two doting males to look after her.

Emily turned around and went back to work, losing herself in the fantasy she was creating. She wasn't sure if she would ever summon the courage to ask James to model for her, but for now, the secret sketch gave her a forbidden thrill.

When the door opened again, she realized she'd lost track of time. "I'll be right there, Corey."

"I'm not Corey," a deep voice said from behind her.

Reacting like the guilty female she was, she closed the sketchbook, took a deep breath and turned to face her fantasy.

He stood before her, with a simple white T-shirt tucked into a pair of frayed and faded jeans. The stitching on the seams was loose and one knee protruded through a threadbare hole. She'd never seen a more handsome man.

"Dinner is ready," he said.

"I'm sorry. I meant to come outside."

"That's okay."

She rose, leaving the sketchbook on her drawing table. He didn't ask what she was working on, but she would have lied anyway. Emotions still ran high between them, the confusion that fueled their relationship evident in every desperate glance, in every awkwardly romantic gesture.

He moved toward her. "I didn't mean to make you cry, Emily."

She wanted to touch him, to smooth the hair that fell onto his forehead, but her hand had begun to tremble, just a little, just enough to make her self-conscious. "That was days ago. Everything is all right now."

"Are you sure? You've been spending a lot of time in here."

Did he think she was avoiding him? She glanced back at her sketchbook. If only he knew. "I'm fine, James."

"Are you getting enough rest?"

"Yes." She still got tired on her feet, but she could

only spend so much time in bed. She knew some patients recovered quicker than others. "I'm a lady of leisure."

He smiled at that. "Then join me for dinner, dear lady."

"I'd be honored, sir." She took the arm he offered and allowed him to escort her to the patio, where their meal and a six-year-old boy waited.

Corey ran to pull back her chair and she knew James had coached him ahead of time. Her brother was learning to be quite a man.

"Thank you, Master Corey." She sat and examined the table. "This looks wonderful." Wildflowers and white candles, she thought. A pan of baked chicken with cream sauce, a bowl of green beans topped with almonds and a salad tossed with exotic greens. She smiled and reached for her napkin. Corey's plate held a boiled hot dog and a side of macaroni and cheese. "I'm impressed."

James sat across from her. "Don't be. The chicken is one of the soup recipes and the green beans were frozen. They came that way."

"I'm still impressed." And touched by the sentiment, by the care he'd taken to prepare her food, by the sheer beauty of eating outdoors on a warm, almost-summer night.

"We got ice cream for dessert." Corey beamed at her. "And chocolate sauce and whipped cream and cherries and everything."

"Then I'll be sure to save room." She leaned over and kissed the top of her brother's head, then proceeded to say a silent grace, thanking God for the gifts she'd been given, for Corey and James and the wonder of being alive.

They talked about simple things over dinner, things to which her brother could relate. Within no time, Corey wolfed down his food and raced into the kitchen to make a cherry-topped dessert. Then he fidgeted with the empty bowl and asked to be excused to watch his favorite sitcom.

Emily granted him permission, and when he was gone, she and James stared at each other from across the table.

"Do you want some ice cream?" he asked.

"Not just yet."

"How about some tea?"

"That sounds good." He offered her a cup of green tea every day, and she'd become accustomed to the mild taste.

"I'll be back in a minute."

He returned in three, with a pretty china cup and a tray with milk and honey. He'd brought himself a bottle of domestic beer. He twisted the cap while she sweetened her drink and took small sips.

"Is this difficult for you?" she asked.

"What?"

"Staying here."

"Why would it be?"

"I thought it was easier for cowboys to be near their work."

He swallowed a swig of his beer. "I'm not that much of a cowboy."

She thought about the black Stetson and battered boots he routinely wore. "You look like a horseman." But he looked like a pierced-and-tattooed city boy, too. Nothing was cut-and-dried where James was concerned.

He glanced up at the sky. "It's a nice night."

"Yes, it is." Rather than look up, she kept her gaze fixed on him. "You made it special."

He caught her watching him. "I enjoy being here with you. And with Corey."

"You're a good influence on him."

"I like kids. I—" James stalled and picked up his beer. He what? Had a son? A little boy he still thought about every day? "I didn't have a stable upbringing," he said instead. "I wasn't raised in a nurturing home." That much he could tell her, that much he wanted her to know.

She came around the table and sat next to him. "This is the first time you've mentioned your family."

"There isn't much to tell. My mom was white and my real dad was Cherokee, but he didn't stick around long enough to matter. So my mom divorced him and married this trashy white guy who used to beat me."

"Oh, James."

Sympathy laced her voice, but he shrugged it off. "When I got big enough, I hit him back." He looked at his hands and recalled the violence. "I hated him. The first time he called me a heathen, I wanted to kill him."

"Is that when you pierced your body?"

He nodded. "I didn't know anything about being Indian, but I'd heard that some of the tribes used to fast and dance and pierce their flesh, offering sacrifice and prayer to the Creator. I wanted to be part of that somehow, so I jammed a needle through my nipple and made a permanent hole in my skin. I was only fourteen, and I needed to do something spiritual. Something my stepfather couldn't take away from me.''

''Who taught you about your heritage?''

''My best friend's uncle. I was running around with another Cherokee boy, and he was just as rebellious as I was. At first, neither one of us gave a damn about our heritage. But we finally decided to learn, especially after my piercing experience. His uncle respected me for that. He understood it.'' James smiled at the memory. ''He also showed me how to care for the wound, to keep it from getting infected.''

Emily traced the outline of the nipple ring through his T-shirt, and they gazed at each other, caught in one of those warm, tender moments.

''Did it hurt?'' she asked.

''Like crazy. And it took about three months to heal.''

''You were a wild child, weren't you, James?''

He almost laughed. He'd robbed the principal's house on the night he'd graduated from high school. ''My mom said I was a bad seed.''

''That's an awful thing for a mother to say.''

''Even if it's true?''

''You're not a bad seed.'' She smoothed the front of his hair. ''You're my champion.''

The compliment made him proud. And sad. And confused. He wasn't a troubled kid anymore. He was a hardened criminal.

Bloody hell, he thought, before he cupped Emily's face and kissed her. Touching her was the only thing that kept him sane, that helped him forget.

She made a kittenish sound and let him take her tongue. She tasted of tea and honey and sips of warm milk, of everything pure and good. When he leaned back to look at her, she gave him an intoxicated smile, like a hummingbird who'd drunk too much nectar.

He owed her the truth, or as much of it as he could manage. "She was my wife, Emily."

She snapped out of her daze. "What?"

"The woman who died from cancer was my wife."

Silence fell. He waited for her to speak, waited through the clock-ticking lull.

"You were married?" she finally said.

"Yes, but not legally. We had a private ceremony. We said vows to each other."

"What was her name?"

He couldn't say it, but he couldn't make up a name, either. James Dalton wasn't supposed to have a wife. He'd broken a WITSEC rule by revealing pertinent information about Reed. "Does it matter? She's gone now."

Emily didn't press the issue, but he suspected she wouldn't. She was too respectful to dishonor the dead.

"We were only together for a few years," he said. "Then she started getting sick, with symptoms that could have been caused by any number of things. We didn't even consider lung cancer." He could feel Emily watching him, latching on to his grief. "She was in her twenties, a nonsmoker. Lung cancer is rare in people under forty."

"How did it happen?" Emily asked. "Why did she get sick?"

"I don't know. It's hard to say. It could have been secondhand smoke. Or she could have been exposed to high levels of radon.'' He finished his beer, hoping to wash away the pain. ''Smoking is the leading cause of lung cancer, but radon causes between fifteen and twenty thousand lung cancer deaths each year.''

''I've heard of it,'' she said. ''It's a gas you can't see or smell. Kind of like carbon monoxide.''

He nodded, recalling how Emily had lost her parents. ''Except people don't die overnight from radon. Lung cancer takes years to develop.'' He frowned at the bottle in his hand. ''The thing that turns my stomach is that I used to smoke. My wife had small cell carcinoma, and there I was, exposing her to second-hand smoke.''

''You didn't know she had cancer, James.''

''It doesn't matter. I'm still partially responsible. Me, her father, her brothers.'' The mobsters trying to kill him, he thought. The bastards running the L.A. mob. ''We all smoked. Everyone she associated with was putting her at risk.''

''How long ago did she die?'' Emily asked.

''It's been a year.'' A long, lonely year, he thought.

''I'm so sorry you lost her. And now I understand why my condition worries you.'' She smiled a little. ''Why you're so determined to take care of me.''

''I couldn't bear to lose you, too.'' He set down the empty bottle. There was a time when he would have smashed it, splintering his skin with shards of glass. Emily had changed that side of him. But that didn't absolve him of his sins. He was still an accessory to murder. And he always would be.

Emily sat next to Diane on the sofa, the midday sun peeking through the blinds. The coffee table held

the lunch they'd prepared—ham and cheese sand-
wiches, potato chips and iced tea.

"You're a genius, Di." Rather than wait for Emily's doctor to supply the news, Diane had suggested
calling the pathology department at the hospital to see
if her biopsy results were in.

Diane reached for her drink. "I figured it was
worth a try. Why wait around for the middleman
when you can go right to the source?"

"The middleman?" Emily laughed. "My doctor is
more than a middleman."

The other woman laughed, too. "You know what
I mean."

Yes, Emily knew. The news she'd received today
was better than winning the lottery. She was truly
cancer-free. Her disease hadn't metastasized. "I can't
wait to tell James."

"So how's it going, anyway?"

"With James?"

"He's living with you. It doesn't get much cozier
than that."

"He's only staying until I recover."

"And?"

"And he told me that what's happening between
us scares him."

Diane moved to the edge of her seat. "So what
exactly is happening?"

Dare she admit it? Say the words keeping her up
at night? She gazed at her friend. She'd never kept
secrets from Diane, and she wasn't about to start now.
"I think I'm in love with him." What else could the
desperation in her heart be? The unwavering ache?
The thrill of holding him, of needing him?

"Is he in love with you?"

"I don't know." Emily twisted the napkin on her lap. "James isn't easy to read." And she didn't want to hope too deeply, to set herself up for destruction.

"I'll bet he is. Why else would he be scared?"

"Because of my cancer." She'd already told Diane about James's wife. "He's been through so much."

"True, but he doesn't have to be afraid anymore. Once he finds out your cancer is gone, he can stop worrying." Diane sent her an optimistic smile. "You two can make a life together. You can have lots of babies." She patted her protruding belly. "Like me."

Emily glanced at her friend's tummy, tempted to imagine herself in the other woman's place. How would it feel to marry James? To cradle his child in her womb? "Don't talk like that, Di. Don't get me started."

"Why not? You just admitted that you loved the guy."

"I know. But James is so complicated." So tortured, she thought. So haunted. "He's like this dark angel just waiting to fall."

Diane made a moonstruck face. "God, that's sexy. A rogue angel. What more could a girl want?"

"Don't tease me." Emily flicked a crust of bread at her friend. She knew Diane was using humor to diffuse her nerves, to make falling in love seem less stressful.

"Come on, Em. You've dreamed about this all your life. Prince Charming finally has a face." The brunette flashed a dastardly grin. "And quite a bod, too."

"He does, doesn't he?" Tall, tan and sculpted with

muscles. She could almost feel the warmth his skin exuded. "I can't wait until I recover. I want to touch him again. I want to put my hands all over him."

"You've got some glorious nights to look forward to. Sex is even better when you're in love."

"Really?" Her desperate heart made an excited leap. She couldn't imagine being more fulfilled, but the romantic notion intrigued her. "Do you think love makes it better for men, too?"

Diane tilted her head, pondering the question. "Probably not. They're horn dogs either way."

They looked at each other and laughed, but by the time Diane departed, Emily had worked herself into an emotional tizzy. Thanks to Diane's well-intentioned meddling, Emily was driving herself nuts with images of happily ever after, with hope-filled wishes and candy-coated dreams.

James came home from work at six-fifteen, wearing a faded shirt, Wrangler jeans, dusty boots and a breathtaking smile.

"Hey," he said by way of a greeting.

"Hey yourself." She followed him into the bedroom, where he kept his clothes. He always showered and changed as soon as he got home. She was becoming accustomed to his habits, even if he was sleeping on the couch.

"Where's Corey?" he asked.

She watched him gather a white T-shirt and a pair of freshly laundered jeans. "Steven's mom took the boys to her husband's softball game."

"They're a great family, aren't they?"

"Yes." But we could be a great family, too, she thought.

"Do you want to get takeout tonight?" he asked as he removed his boots.

"Sure." She couldn't help but smile. James usually discussed dinner while he rifled through his underwear drawer. She'd given him a portion of her dresser, and he was surprisingly tidy, keeping his belongings in order.

"I'll be back in a flash." He pressed a sweet kiss to her forehead and headed to the bathroom, leaving her with a big, tender ache.

She sat on the edge of the bed and listened to the sound of the shower running. She knew he would emerge with his jeans fastened low on his hips and his hair falling in towel-dried disarray.

Emily reached for Dee-Dee and stroked the bear's matted head. Should she confide in James? Admit that she loved him?

Yes, she thought. She should. But not now. Not this soon. The best she could do was tell him about her biopsy results.

Five minutes later James returned, looking the way she'd imagined—clean and damp and undeniably male.

She rose to meet him, to tip her head and gaze up at him. "I have some news."

He cupped her cheek. "What is it, baby?"

"My test results came in." She gave him a strong, steady smile. "It's over. The cancer is gone."

His voice quavered. "No lymph node detection?"

"No."

"Oh, God." He pulled her tight against him, so close she could feel his heart pounding against hers.

When he stepped back to look at her, his eyes,

those tortured eyes, actually sparkled. "We have to celebrate, Emily. As soon as your leg heals, we'll go out. We'll drink and eat and dance."

"And have sex," she added. "The best sex imaginable."

"That's my girl." He laughed, and she practically flung herself into his embrace.

He spun her around, and she inhaled his soap-and-shampoo scent. He smelled like the forest on a breezy day, like wood smoke and musk, like tall, sturdy trees, like sprigs of mint.

She closed her eyes, and he kissed her, filling her with warmth and wonder. And when he lifted her into his arms and made her sigh, she prayed that he loved her, too.

Nine

Someone touched him—a warm, soft hand skimming his forehead, smoothing his hair away from his face. James shifted on the couch. Was he dreaming?

The living room was dark, except for a slice of moonlight slipping in through lace curtains, making a haunting pattern on the wall.

Hadn't he been watching TV? Reclining on the sofa, with his head on Emily's lap?

"I fell asleep," he said, realizing she was still there, holding him.

"Just for a little while." Her voice was as soft as her touch.

He tilted his head back to look at her, but she was a silhouette in the dark. She must have turned off the television with the remote, making the room quiet and still. "You should go to bed."

"I want to stay here."

He wanted her to stay, too. "Then we should switch places. This has to be uncomfortable for you."

"I'm fine. I like holding you."

His Emily, he thought. His sweet, perfect Emily. A week had passed since she'd told him about her biopsy results, and he thanked the Creator every day for keeping her safe.

"I'm going to tell Corey that you and I are a couple," she said. "That we're boyfriend and girlfriend."

Her description of their relationship made him smile. She made them sound like teenagers from the fifties, sock-hop dancers going steady. But they weren't, of course. They were consenting adults—lovers from a modern, fast-paced, overly violent world.

"I miss being with you, Emily."

She leaned over to kiss him. And when she did, her hair fell forward, draping him like a satin quilt. Her mouth was warm and willing, her tongue moist and inviting. The kiss tasted of passion, of pleasure, of summer nights and sultry dreams.

She moved back to catch her breath. "It won't be long before we can make love again."

"I wasn't talking about sex." He tried not to think about sex too much, to arouse his system before she was ready. To lust that deeply, to crave what he couldn't have. "I was talking about sleeping in your room. Just being with you."

"I miss that, too." Her tone turned wistful. "After I tell Corey about us, you can stay with me. I want my brother to understand what's going on. It wouldn't be proper for him to walk into my room one morning and find you in my bed. I need to talk to him first.''

James suspected she would recite a fairy-tale version of the birds and the bees. Romantic, innocent stuff a six-year-old could comprehend. ''You're raising him right. Corey is going to grow into a respectable young man someday.''

''That's all I can hope for.''

In the silence that followed, he gazed at the ghostly shadows on the wall. Was the moon slipping behind the trees, drifting in a starless sky? He closed his eyes and wished he had more to offer Emily. That he was worthy of her and Corey.

She combed her fingers through his hair. He remained on the couch, his head on her lap. He'd rarely spent this kind of time with Beverly. Falling asleep in front of the TV would have been a luxury in those days. A luxury a man on the run couldn't afford.

''I'm still scared,'' he said.

''Of what's happening between us?''

''Yes.'' He opened his eyes and studied the shadows again. They were shifting, he noticed. Changing form. He thought he saw a crow but the birdlike shape disappeared before he could latch on to it.

''So am I,'' she said. ''But it's a good kind of scared.''

Her admission thrust a ball of panic straight to his stomach. Good? How could her attachment to a criminal be good?

He sat up and turned on a low-burning lamp, flooding the room with a golden hue. Her image came into view, like a mist-veiled mirage. Her nightgown was gray and smoky, her skin was translucent, her arms were pale and delicately boned.

"I've been waiting for you to bring this up." She reached for a throw pillow and hugged it to her chest. "All week, I've been hoping and praying that you'd say something."

"Why?"

"Because I love you."

His chest constricted, trapping him between turmoil and tenderness. All along, he'd wanted to steal her heart. The thief in him had wanted to take her most valuable possession.

"This is my fault," he said.

"It's not anyone's fault, James. It just happened." She hugged the pillow a little tighter. "Diane thinks you love me, too. But I'm never sure about anything, not with you."

He wanted to comfort her, to calm her fears. But he stood instead, jamming his hands into his pockets. "I'm never sure about myself, either."

"You've been through some difficult times. You lost your wife. It can't be easy to have feelings for someone again."

But I do, he thought. He had feelings he couldn't control. "If I tell you that I love you, too, it won't make a difference. I'll still be scared."

Her gaze locked on to his. Her eyes shone like faceted jewels, maintaining the brilliance, the luster of a lost treasure.

"Do you?" she asked.

He dug his hands deeper into his pockets. He couldn't lie to her. He'd told enough lies already. And lying to himself wouldn't solve anything, either. He'd been in love before. He knew the signs, the symptoms that never went away.

"Yes," he said.

"You love me?"

"Yes." Did she want him to sign an oath? A declaration in blood?

Her hopeful eyes were still locked on to his. "You honest-to-goodness love me?"

"Yes, damn it. I love you. But I feel like a bull that's about to be branded, so don't make any sudden moves."

She laughed and leaped to her feet, nearly tripping over the coffee table.

"Watch your leg," he cautioned. She'd been bouncing around too much lately, putting pressure on a wound that had yet to heal. "If you pop a stitch—"

She ignored his warning and threw her arms around his neck. He gave up and held her, nuzzling her neck, inhaling the spring-meadow scent of her hair.

"This doesn't change anything," he said.

"It changes everything." She put her head on his shoulder. "It gives us a place to start. A new beginning."

Did it? He wrapped her in a protective hug and prayed she was right. But deep down, he knew she wasn't.

What kind of "new beginning" would they have

if his security were breached? If the mob caught up with him? If James Dalton disappeared one day and never came back?

James pulled into the parking lot of a hamburger joint located between Silver Wolf and Lewiston. He spotted Zack Ryder's black sedan and blew an anxious, stomach-clenching breath. For the past two days, James could barely eat, barely sleep. There was no one to talk to, no one to confide in, except Ryder.

A man he didn't particularly like.

The WITSEC inspector waited in his car. James opened the passenger door and climbed in. For a moment, neither spoke. Ryder sipped coffee from a plastic cup. He wore casual clothes, a tan shirt and jeans. He didn't look like a cop. But he was, James thought. Ryder was a lawman, through and through.

"Do you want some coffee, Dalton? Or a burger or something?"

"No, thanks."

Ryder turned to face him. "So, what gives? Are you having woman trouble? Feeling guilty about that little blonde?"

James glared at him. It already chapped his hide that he had to spill his guts to a cop, and Ryder's annoying ability to probe his mind only made matters worse. "How do you know about Emily? I never told you I was seeing her. I never even told you she lived in Silver Wolf."

"Strange coincidence, isn't it? You and her ending up in the same town."

"Yeah. And apparently Big Brother is watching every damn thing I do."

"Don't get defensive." Ryder took an unaffected sip of his coffee. "It's my job to keep you alive. And I can't do that if I don't nose into your activities now and then."

James studied the other man's hard, chiseled features. "Are you a traditional Indian?"

The inspector shook his head. "No."

"Me, neither."

"I know."

Of course, he knew. The son of a bitch knew everything. "Is that the only thing we have in common?"

"Probably. Deputy marshals and former mobsters make strange bedfellows." Ryder gave him a blasé look, and suddenly, they both laughed.

Their relationship was absurd. And more important than James had realized.

In the silence that followed, he gazed out the windshield. He could see the highway, the road leading back to Silver Wolf. "She's in love with me." He paused to spike a hand through his hair. "And I'm in love with her."

"And?"

"And I don't know what the hell I'm supposed to do. How can I make a commitment to a woman who doesn't even know who I am?"

"She knows who you are. She knows you're James Dalton."

"That feels like a sham. I feel like a sham." He turned away from the windshield, away from that fateful road. "I told Emily about my wife. Not her name and who her family is, but I told her that I had a wife who died from cancer.''

Ryder blew out a windy breath. ''And now you want to tell her the rest. You want to tell her about Reed.''

His heart banged against his chest. The idea of telling the woman he loved that he was a former mobster made him ill, but not telling her made him hate himself more than he already did. ''She has a right to know what kind of man I am.''

The inspector didn't agree. ''So you're in love? So you're getting emotionally attached to a beautiful woman? You have to consider the future. What if it doesn't work out? What if you marry her and somewhere down the line she wants a divorce? What if you do something to piss her off? A disgruntled spouse can run to the mob for revenge.''

''She would never do that.''

''How the hell would you know? You've been involved with her for what? A month?''

James bit back his temper. Emily would never hurt him; she would never turn him over to the mob. ''I can't keep lying to her. I can't stand it.''

''You knew the rules when you entered this program.''

''So if I tell her, you're going to kick me out?''

The inspector gave him a level stare. ''No.''

James found the strength to smile. ''No?''

Ryder didn't return the smile. ''You wouldn't be the first witness to tell his or her lover the truth. And you won't be the last, I suppose. But why you're so damned determined to come clean is beyond me.''

"I'll make sure she understands the risk."

"You damn well better."

"I will," James said. "And I'll keep you informed. I'll call you afterward."

Ryder reached for the cigarette pack on the dashboard, slipped one out and struck a match. A second later, he watched James through a haze of smoke. "So when are you going to do it?"

"When?" His nerves began to tangle. "Soon. The sooner the better."

"Today, then?" The inspector dragged on his cigarette. "I wonder what she'll say. It's going to be a hell of a shock."

James shifted in his seat. Was Ryder trying to psych him out? Make him change his mind? When the vehicle started closing in, he grabbed the door handle and bolted, desperate for some air.

Ryder gave him a minute, then exited the car. James leaned against the trunk, his limbs not quite steady. He could feel the other man analyzing him, wondering if he would actually go through with it.

"I have to," he said.

"Then I hope it works out, Dalton. I hope you find what you're looking for. Peace. Redemption. Whatever it is, I hope you find it."

So do I, James thought, as he cursed Reed Blackwood. So do I.

James entered Emily's house through the back door. After his meeting with Ryder, he'd gone to Tandy Stables to catch up on some paperwork and fill in for a ranch hand who'd taken ill. And now his day was over.

Or almost over, he amended, his nerves tangling again.

"James!" The instant he passed the utility room and walked into the kitchen, Corey ran to greet him.

"Hey, partner." He scooped the boy up. Wispy blond bangs framed his eyes, and streaks of dirt stained his cheeks. "Been playing in the yard?"

"Uh-huh." Corey wrinkled his nose. "I had to wear that girly goop again."

"Corbin Taylor Chapman." Emily entered the kitchen and caused James's heart to stop. "Don't you dare complain."

The child made a dramatic face, and James gazed at Emily. She sent him a sweet smile, and he clung to Corey, shifting the child in his arms. Did she love him enough to accept Reed Blackwood? To let a man like Reed remain in her life? To help raise her brother?

Emily came forward to brush James's mouth with a tender kiss. He returned the kiss, and Corey made a silly smooching sound. James wanted to latch on to Emily and never let go, but she was already stepping back, already pinching her brother for teasing them.

James set Corey on his feet and plunked his hat on the boy's head. The Stetson teetered, and the kid looked up at him and grinned.

"Know what?" Corey said.

"No? What?"

"Diane is having a birthday party for Emmy. With balloons and a cake and everything."

"A party?" He searched Emily's gaze. "When's your birthday?"

"June twentieth. I'm having my stitches removed on Friday, so I'll be fine by then. Almost ready to go back to work."

"And I'll be out of school," Corey piped in, watching the adults beneath the brim of the flip-flopping hat. "So I'll get to help, making decorations and stuff. Right, Emmy?"

"That's right." She returned her attention to James. "I like the idea of having a party this year. I have a lot to celebrate. More than just my birthday."

"Of course you do. We all do." He did his damnedest to conceal his emotions, to hide his anxiety. How could he tell her about Reed now? How could he spoil her party?

He would wait to tell her, he thought. Wait until her special celebration was over. He released a ragged breath and decided he better call Ryder later and explain that his plan had been delayed. "What do you want for your birthday?"

"You," she said, making him warm all over.

"That's dumb." Corey interrupted. He'd been told about their romance, but he didn't quite understand the specifics. "You can't have a person for your birthday. It's supposed to be something you can wrap."

James couldn't help but laugh. "I would look pretty goofy with a bow on top of my head."

Emily and Corey laughed, too. James prayed moments like these were his to keep, that he wasn't setting himself up for a fall.

"Can I go back outside?" Corey asked his sister.

"That's fine," she told him. "But try to stay in the shade."

"Okay. Can I keep your hat, James? I'm gonna play cowboy."

"Be my guest, partner. All cowboys need hats."

"Thanks." The boy steadied the Stetson and tore off, leaving James and Emily alone.

"I can take you to the doctor on Friday," he said. "I'm supposed to work, but Lily Mae has been flexible with my schedule."

"That would be great." Emily studied her lover's expression, his taunt mouth, the tiny lines near his eyes. "You're still scared, aren't you?"

He jammed his hands into his pockets, a nervous habit she'd seen him do many times before.

"I'm fine," he said.

"You haven't been sleeping well."

"I've always been a bit of an insomniac."

"I didn't know that." But there was a lot she didn't know about him. They were still learning about each other, she supposed. "When's your birthday, James?"

He didn't answer right away. He glanced at the floor, then shifted his stance. "November fifth."

She stepped a little closer. "I'm sorry this is so difficult for you." That being in love made him so uncomfortable. "It's like a dream for me. I woke up this morning and realized this is the happiest I've ever been in my life."

"Really?" He removed his hands from his pockets.

She reached for him and he wrapped her in a heart-pounding embrace. Were his feelings as deep as hers?

When he touched her, she was convinced they were. But whenever she looked into those haunted eyes, she feared she would lose him.

"Tell me what you want for your birthday," he said.

She inhaled his earthy scent, the horse-and-hay redolence that clung to his clothes. "I already told you."

He smoothed a hand down her hair. "Funny girl. Now tell me something I can buy."

"It doesn't matter." Just knowing that he was part of her life was enough.

"Is the party going to be here or at Diane's house?"

"At Diane's." She burrowed against his chest. "You can invite Lily Mae. And I'll invite Harvey. Wouldn't it be cute to see them together?"

"Cute?" He stepped back. "To watch them bicker all night?"

"To set them up. To play matchmaker." She couldn't stand the thought of Lily Mae and Harvey pining for each other. "You said they were lovers once."

"Probably fifty years ago."

"That's a long time to miss someone." She took his hands and held them. "It's the least we could do."

"The least we could do is mind our own business."

"Spoilsport." She released his hands, but he pulled her back into his arms.

"Fine. I'll invite Lily Mae. But I'm not taking part in any matchmaking scheme."

"Yes, you are."

"No, I'm not."

"It's going to be my birthday. My party." She softened her voice. "You'll have to listen to me then."

He sighed, and she knew she'd won. But only for the moment. With James, nothing was certain. He was truly a shape-shifter—her dark-winged, rebellious protector. The man she loved, but hadn't begun to understand.

Ten

"**T**ell me again why we're here?" James asked as he opened the motel room door on Friday afternoon.

"We're here because I want to see where you slept that night." The night they'd met, Emily thought.

"Women." He shook his head and tossed the key card onto the dresser. "I drive you to Lewiston for a doctor appointment and we end up on a trip down memory lane." He turned around and smiled, the back of his head reflected in the mirror. "You're going to seduce me, aren't you? That's what this is all about."

She scanned the bed and noticed the simple blue quilt. "Maybe."

"Maybe? We just paid sixty-nine bucks for a few hours in a motel room and she says 'Maybe'?"

Emily knew he was teasing her, but she knew he

was anxious to make love, too. To touch and kiss and climax in her arms, to purge his emotions in a hot, desperate release. James was still troubled. In spite of his smile, she could see the ever-present pain in his eyes. "Tell me what you did when you left my room that night."

"What could I do? I came back here." He frowned at the bed, his voice turning rough. "I paced for a while. I—"

"What?" she asked.

"Thought about you."

Her pulse jumped to her throat. "You did?"

"Of course I did." He leaned against the dresser, his shoulders tense. "I was lonely. I wanted to be with you, but I knew it wasn't right."

Emily pictured him, stalking the perimeters of his confinement, his scuffed and battered boots treading the carpet. "I thought about you, too. I couldn't get you off my mind."

He dragged a hand through his hair, tousling the thick, dark strands. "We were strangers. It wasn't meant to happen. Not that night."

In some ways, they were still strangers, she thought. "I want to make new memories. For both of us."

"Are those memories part of my seduction?" he asked, watching her with a hopeful expression.

"Yes." She moved forward. He was still leaning against the dresser. She reached for him, and he held her. Gently, so gently, her heart ached for more. Being this close to him intensified her need to be with him, to take shelter in his arms. They hadn't made love since her surgery, and she missed him terribly.

She reached for the buttons on his shirt, working them free. Then she bared his chest and pressed her lips to his skin. He was strong and solid and warm. She could almost feel his blood rushing through his veins. Her lover, she thought. Her angel. He'd helped her through the most difficult time of her life, insisting the scar on her leg was a badge of courage.

"I'll always be safe with you," she said.

James stroked her hair and felt his hand tremble. "Safe?" With an ex-con? An accessory to murder? A witness hiding from the mob?

"You're my protector," she told him. "My guardian."

When she nuzzled his neck, he absorbed her words, clinging to the illusion that he was worthy of her. He didn't want to think about his past, about the sins he'd committed. Not while she touched him, not while she made his heart yearn for hers.

He opened her blouse, treasuring the warmth of her body, the feel of her skin next to his. Her bra was a wisp of cotton and lace. He could see her nipples through the pale pink fabric.

"I love you," he said. Whatever else happened, he wanted her to know that, to feel it.

"I love you, too." She nearly melted in his arms, and he realized how deeply his words had affected her, how much she needed to hear them.

He scooped her up and carried her to bed. For now, he would be the man she believed him to be, her white knight, her protector.

"It's perfect, isn't it?" she said. "This room. Us. The new memories."

"Yes." He knelt beside her on the bed, slipping off her shoes, removing her pants, fisting the condom she'd tucked into her pocket, sliding it under a pillow. His clothes came next—his jeans, his boots, the shirt she'd unbuttoned.

When they were naked, they touched each other, exploring curves and planes and quivering muscles. She traced his tattoo; he skimmed a hand over her scar. She roamed his chest, and he rubbed between her legs, arousing her, making her arch and sigh.

Her climax was soft and sweet, a flutter of feminine shivers, a breathy pant, an intoxicated smile. He watched it happen, pleased that his touch could make her dreamy.

"You look so pretty." Her hair fanned across the pillow, and her cheeks were flushed. Almost as pink as her nipples.

She rolled over. And suddenly, she straddled his lap, pressing against the hardness. "How do I look now?"

"Gorgeous," he rasped, before he thrust his tongue into her mouth.

The kiss was rough, laden with hunger, with the need to possess. She reached under his pillow and palmed the foil packet. Then she tore it open and fitted him with the condom. Anxious, he waited.

She lifted her hips and impaled herself. Slow, shallow, erotic, maddening. James wasn't sure he would survive. Desperate, he grabbed her waist, pushed her down, felt that warm, wet friction.

"More," he whispered. "All the way."

Sleek and smooth, she rode him, setting the rhythm, the heart-stopping pace. He had to remind himself to breathe, to suck air into his lungs.

She tipped her head back, and her body arched and flowed. Mesmerized, he watched her. She could have been a witch. She could have been a fairy. He didn't know where her magic had come from, but it was there, swirling like mist, falling like rain.

His lady. His love. He reared up to kiss her, to hold her, to plunge deep. To look into her eyes and lose his soul.

"It's good for the soul."

"I'm sorry. What?" Caught off guard, James turned. He hadn't heard Diane's husband approach, which meant he was zoning out. Ned Kerr wasn't a quiet man. He walked with a heavy foot and spoke in a strong, friendly voice.

"Nature is good for the soul." Ned indicated the view of the river from his front yard.

"Yes, it is." Moonlight baptized the water with silver-crested currents, and stars reflected the night sky.

"Are you enjoying the party?" Ned asked.

James nodded. Festive sounds drifted from the house, where Emily's birthday celebration was in full swing. "It's a great party. It was nice of you and Diane to do this."

"Emily is going to be our son's godmother." Ned flashed a proud smile. "Diane told you we're having a boy, didn't she?"

"Yes, she did." James thought about his own son, about the little boy he'd left behind. "When the early Cherokee inquired about the sex of a new arrival, they used to ask, 'Is it a bow or a sifter?' A meal sifter," he clarified. "Boys made bows for their arrows and girls beat corn into meal."

Ned chuckled. "Then it's a bow. But don't tell Diane about the meal-sifter thing. She'll probably think it's sexist. You know, women's lib and all that."

Just then, Diane's voice sounded from behind them. "Did I hear my name?"

"That woman has ears like radar," her husband mumbled.

"I heard that." She tried to slip her arms around the back of Ned's waist, but her protruding tummy got in the way. "I heard all of it."

"So did I," another feminine voice said.

James looked over and saw Emily. She smiled at him, and his heart bumped his chest. "I was just getting some air," he said.

"And discussing gender differences with Ned." She laughed and came forward. "Does this mean I'm a sifter?"

"I think we should make them beat corn into meal," Diane suggested.

"Told ya." Ned switched places with his wife, putting his arms around her waist, cradling their unborn child. "Women's lib."

James watched the other couple, envying the simplicity of their lifestyle, the easy, everyday happiness they were destined to share.

Emily interrupted his thoughts. "So am I?"

"You don't like being a sifter?" He reached out to grab her, to make her squeal. "Would you rather be bread? There's another Cherokee baby-gender saying that asks, 'Is it ballsticks or bread?'"

She raised her eyebrows. "Ballsticks?"

"Like the game. Stickball." He laughed and hugged her. "At least that's what I think it means."

"You think?" She gave him a quick, lust-driven kiss and made his pulse race.

"None of that," Diane chided. "We've still got a party going on."

"Speaking of which." Emily dragged James toward the house. "It's time to play matchmaker."

He winced, realizing she hadn't given up on the Harvey/Lily Mae scheme. "Where are they?"

"In the basement. At opposite ends of the room, watching other people dance." She led him through a crowded kitchen and down the basement steps, where country music played on a state-of-the-art sound system.

"See?" Emily guided him to a buffet laden with finger foods. "Harvey's over there. And Lily Mae's sorting through Ned's CD collection. I'll bet she's just dying to dance. Go tell Harvey to ask her."

"Me?" James grabbed a stalk of celery filled with cream cheese. "Why don't you tell him?"

"Because you're a man, and you should say something about how pretty she looks."

"She's my boss." He glanced at Lily Mae with her gray-streaked hair and sun-baked skin. "My sixty-eight-year-old boss."

"She's still pretty." Emily snagged the celery out of his hand before he could take a bite.

"All right. Fine." At this point, he didn't have the heart to deny the birthday girl her wish. "But don't blame me if this doesn't work."

"It will." Confident, she gave him a sweet little push.

James walked around the swaying couples. He supposed the music was romantic enough for a matchmaking scheme, but he wasn't sure if Harvey Osborn would agree. The retired postal worker stood with his arms crossed. As usual, he wore a pair of suspenders and baggy pants.

"Hey, Harvey," James said. "Do you like the music?"

"I've always enjoyed country. What about you?"

"I like all sorts of music." James glanced at Emily and saw her watching him from the buffet table, eating his celery stick. "Lily Mae certainly looks nice this evening."

Harvey shot his gaze across the room. "She's always been a mite skinny for my tastes."

"Really? I saw pictures of her when she was young. She looked pretty good to me." The old man narrowed his eyes, and James realized he'd hit a jealous streak. "Damn good, in fact."

Harvey made an indignant sound. "She's a nutcase, that one. Crazy as a loon."

James decided to pull out all the stops, to use his cheating, criminal charm. "I'll bet you could tame her. A practical man like you is what a woman like Lily Mae needs."

Suddenly the retired postal worker stood a little taller. "I suppose I could. If I wanted to."

"She talks about you all the time."

"Does she?" Harvey nearly snapped his suspenders. "And what does she say?"

That you're on old goat, James thought, biting back a smile. "This and that. You know Lily Mae. She tends to babble."

"That she does."

"You should ask her to dance."

Harvey's head whipped around. "Now? In front of all these people?"

"I'll bet you're a good dancer."

"I certainly was in my day."

"Then there you go." When Lily Mae turned around, James used her eye contact as leverage. "She can't quit looking at you, Harvey. It's pathetic."

"I suppose I could give the old bird a thrill."

As Harvey shuffled across the room to approach Lily Mae, James shifted to grin at Emily. She saluted him with a finger sandwich and he imagined kissing her breathless.

A few seconds later, they sat on a sofa in the basement and watched Harvey and Lily Mae dance.

"It's a damn good thing she didn't turn him down," James said.

"She wouldn't dare." Emily fed him a grape from her plate. "Not after the spiel I gave her earlier."

He swallowed the grape and reached for an olive. "What spiel?"

"I told her that Harvey has been trying to work up

the nerve to ask her to dance all night. And that you were going to give him a confidence booster.''

''You little devil. You conned her. And me.''

''Did I?'' She batted her lashes and made him laugh.

He gazed at the older couple again. ''I'll bet they're going to be bickering by the time the party ends.''

''Maybe.'' She put her head on his shoulder. ''But at least now they have a chance.''

Do we have a chance? he wondered. Or would Reed destroy their future? ''Here.'' He reached into his jacket pocket to hand her a small, gift-wrapped box.

Like a wide-eyed child, she tore into it, discovering a gold locket he'd purchased at an antique store.

''There's a message inside,'' he told her.

She opened the locket and gazed at the words he'd written on a small scrap of paper. Then she read them out loud. ''You will be unable to glance away. Your thought is not to wander…I have just come to draw away your soul.''

''It's part of a Cherokee incantation.'' He touched her cheek, absorbing the warmth of her skin. ''A spell of attraction. I think about it whenever you look at me. Whenever we look at each other.''

Her eyes filled with tears. ''I love you, James Dalton.''

''I love you, too,'' he said, knowing that tomorrow he would have to tell her the truth—that his name wasn't really James Dalton.

Emily awakened the next morning to find James watching her. Fighting grogginess, she stretched and blinked, then noticed how intense he looked.

When didn't he look intense? she asked herself.

He reached for her hair, smoothing several stray pieces away from her face. "Hey, sleepyhead."

She glanced at the clock and smiled, grateful he'd touched her. "It's still early." And they had hours to relax, to lounge in bed. She knew Corey would sleep in. He'd stayed up late last night, running around the party with Steven, having the time of his life. "How about some coffee? And maybe some toast and jam?"

"If you're hungry."

"I am, but I'd like to eat in bed."

"I can fix it," he offered.

Emily grabbed her robe and slipped it over her nightgown. "That's okay. I need to get back into the swing of being a waitress." She gave him a quick kiss and headed to the kitchen.

Enjoying her task, she started a pot of coffee and set a loaf of white bread on the counter. She knew James liked his coffee dark and his toast light and golden.

Maybe she should scramble some eggs, too. And pan-fry several slices of ham. Bustling around the kitchen, she cooked breakfast and prepared a festive-looking tray, garnishing their plates with sprigs of parsley and carefully sliced orange wedges.

Finally, she carried their meal into the bedroom and placed it on the dresser.

"That looks good," James said. "More than I expected."

"I was in the mood to fuss." And she adored this

domestic feeling, the cozy comfort of sharing her room with James, of seeing him in his boxers every morning.

She handed him his coffee and he took a small sip and set it on the nightstand on his side of the bed. Balancing his plate on his lap, he reached for a napkin and a fork. Emily began to eat, as well. After she devoured her ham and started on her eggs, she noticed her appetite was much stronger than his. But breakfast had been her idea.

Lost in thought, she fingered the locket James had given her. The words from the Cherokee incantation were secured inside it, where they would remain. Next to her heart, she thought. Emily intended to wear the necklace every day.

Dreamy, she picked up her toast and took a bite. Then she turned and saw James gazing at her with that intense expression.

"We need to talk," he said.

"About what?"

He set his plate aside. "Us. Me. Our future."

She looked directly into his eyes, and when he glanced away, she knew something was terribly wrong. He wasn't supposed to avoid her gaze. He wasn't supposed to break the spell.

"I'm sorry, Emily."

"For what?" Fearful, she clutched the locket. Had he changed his mind? Had he decided that loving her was too complicated? That their relationship was too committed?

"I'm sorry for everything."

"Don't do this, James."

He released an audible breath. "First of all, my name isn't James Dalton and I wasn't born on November fifth. My real name is Reed Blackwood, and I was born on September second." He reached for his coffee and wrapped his hands around the mug. "I'm an ex-con. A high-dollar thief and an electronics expert." He took a sip and swallowed hard. "I'm also a former member of the West Coast Family, a Los Angeles–based mob."

Confused, she merely stared at him. "Is this some sort of joke? An after-birthday gag?"

"I wish it were."

Refusing to believe him, she reached across the bed and grabbed his wallet from the nightstand. She'd never looked through his personal belongings before, never seen his license, his social security number. "James Dalton," she read the name on each item, then tossed them onto the sheet. "Are these fake? Is all of this a lie?"

"The government gave me that identity. I'm—"

"What? Some sort of spy? First you're a crook and now you're—"

"I'm in the Witness Protection Program, Emily. And I'm not even supposed to be telling you this."

Panic gripped her hard and fast. "You testified against someone?"

He nodded.

"Who? The L.A. mob? There's no such thing. There can't be."

"There is. And if they find me, they'll kill me."

"And you're here? In my home? With my brother?" Tears filled her eyes. She couldn't think, couldn't breathe, couldn't keep her pulse from pounding in her head. "Is Corey in danger? Would they kidnap him to get to you?" Without waiting for an answer, she tore off, rushing to her brother's room.

When she opened the door, she saw Corey sleeping soundly in his bed, his fingers curled around the blanket. In the next instant, she heard James come up behind her.

"They won't hurt Corey," he said. "And they won't hurt you."

She closed her brother's door and turned to meet James's gaze. This time, he didn't glance away.

"But they'll keep searching for you?" she asked.

"Yes."

"To kill you?"

"Yes," he said again, leaving her knees and her heart much too weak.

Eleven

————

Emily moved away from Corey's door, and James realized she was concerned the boy would awaken, that he would overhear their conversation.

"I need to sit down." She returned to her room, and James followed, wondering what in God's name to say next. He could see that he'd frightened her.

And rightly so. Who wouldn't be afraid?

She sat on the edge of the bed and twisted the belt on her robe. James glanced at her half-eaten breakfast. She'd nearly dumped her plate when she'd dashed out of the room to check on her brother.

"The mobsters who are after me don't prey on innocent people," he said. "If they did, I would have never gotten involved with you. I would never put you or Corey in danger."

"But what about you? I don't want you to die, James."

"WITSEC promised to protect me."

"WITSEC?"

"Witness Protection, Witness Security, it's the same thing. But you can't repeat any of this. Not to anyone. Not even Diane."

Tears welled in her eyes. "I won't. I swear, I won't. I would never jeopardize your safety."

A stretch of silence spanned between them, and James wondered where to begin. Uneasy, he remained standing, his thoughts spinning like a spider weaving a complicated web. "I'm not from Oklahoma. I was born in Austin, Texas, and when I was twelve, my family moved to a small town in the Texas Hill Country."

"Is anything you told me about your family true?"

He shoved his hands in his pockets. "The part about my stepdad beating me is true."

"And your mother?"

"That was true, too. But I have a half sister I never told you about. Her name is Heather, but she's white so we don't look anything alike." He paused to clear his throat. "She's the only person who ever loved me. Besides my wife." He paused again. "And you."

Emily lifted her gaze. "Your wife is real?"

"Yes."

"And her cancer was real?"

"Yes." And so was her grave, he thought. The resting place he'd never been allowed to visit. "My wife's name was Beverly Halloway. And her father is head of the West Coast Family. Or he was, before he went to prison. His sons took over. But they want me dead, too.''

Her face went pale. ''Your wife's family runs the mob that's trying to kill you?''

James blew a tight breath. ''They never wanted me to be with her in the first place.''

''Yet you were part of their organization.''

''I botched some orders I was given and they stopped trusting me.'' What would Emily say when she discovered he was more than a thief? That he'd been part of a murder scheme that had gone awry? ''There was no way they were going to let me marry the boss's daughter. I was warned to stay away from her.''

She stopped fidgeting with her robe, and he walked around to the other side of the bed, picked up his cup and took a sip. When the coffee hit his stomach in an acidic burn, he set it back down. ''Beverly and I were planning to elope, but her family got to me first. They sent a couple of guys over to my place to beat the crap out of me.''

She reached for her teddy bear and held it, and the nervous, childlike gesture made him ache.

''What happened?'' she asked.

''Halloway's goons messed me up pretty bad. I was unconscious for a while, then Beverly found me. She and my sister got me out of town. They nursed my wounds, and the three of us ended up on the run.''

She hugged the bear a little closer. ''For how long?''

''A year and a half. The mob sent a hit man after

us. His job was to kill me and take Beverly back to her father.''

"What about your sister?"

"Heather couldn't go home, not without the mob tracing her whereabouts back to me. So she stayed with us." Running, he thought. Moving from state to state, living like a fugitive. "Beverly got sick when we were on the run. Everything changed after we found out she had cancer. We knew it was over."

"I'm sorry," she said.

He leaned against the dresser. There was still more, so much more, to say. "I have a child, Emily. Beverly and I had a son."

For a moment, she simply stared at him. He waited through the silence, waited while his heart banged against his chest.

Finally, she spoke. "What's his name?"

"Justin."

"Where is he?"

"After we found out that Beverly had cancer, we gave Justin to my sister. We asked her to raise him, to tell everyone that he was hers. It was the only way to keep Beverly's family from knowing his true parentage. We didn't want the Halloways trying to get custody of him."

"I don't understand." She set the teddy bear on the bed. "I thought your sister was white. How could she pass off your son as hers?"

"Heather had an Indian lover, and she was pregnant by him. She was only a few months along when she got tangled up in my mess." Memories clouded his mind, taking him back in time. "I was on the run with two pregnant women. But the mob didn't know.'' The memories got thicker, darker, more painful as he went on. ''Justin was born first. A week later, Heather had a son. But he was stillborn. The umbilical cord was wrapped around his neck. He was just this little thing, all scrawny and blue. He wasn't breathing. I couldn't get him to breathe.''

Emily's voice broke. ''Oh, James.''

''We were still hiding out from the mob, holed up in this tiny cabin in Oklahoma, and that's where both babies were born. We were too afraid to go to a hospital, to risk getting caught. But we should have.''

''It's over now. You can't go back.''

''I know.'' He'd mourned his sister's child. He'd cried and prayed and buried the infant in a makeshift coffin, sprinkling the unmarked grave with sage.

''How did all of this end?'' she asked.

''I knew the mob would never quit looking for me, so I kept running. Since Beverly was too sick to stay on the road, Heather took her back to her father. Halloway had the money to get her the medical treatment she needed, to hire a private nurse, to make her death less painful.'' James glanced at the window, at the summer sun drifting into the room. ''By then, Justin was already ten months old, and Heather had agreed to be his mother. After she took Beverly home, she went back to her lover in Texas and asked him to raise my son. To pretend Justin was his.''

''And he agreed?''

''Yes. Heather's lover was my friend.''

''The Cherokee boy you mentioned from your youth?''

James nodded. "We were like brothers once. He'll be good to my son."

"So Justin will never know that you're his father?"

"No. But that was my choice. My way of giving him a normal life, of keeping the Halloways away from him."

"How did you get into the Witness Protection Program, James? How did you escape the mob?"

"While I was still on the run, the FBI got in touch with my sister, and she made contact with me. The feds said they might be able to cut me a deal, to hook me up with WITSEC. Of course, that meant testifying against Beverly's dad and some of his crew. But at that point, Beverly was already dead. I knew it wouldn't affect her."

"You did the right thing. The Halloways sound like awful people."

"I was an awful person, too."

She shook her head. "Not like them."

"How would you know?"

"Because they hire hit men to kill people. You were a thief, but you're not a murderer. You would never do that. You would never take someone else's life."

She came toward him, and his feet froze to the floor. Suddenly he couldn't tell her. He couldn't admit that he was an accessory to murder. But he hadn't told Beverly, either. His wife had died without knowing the truth.

"It'll be okay," Emily said. "We'll get through this."

How could they? he asked himself. How could they

live in the shadow of his lie? Of the sin he couldn't bear to confess?

She put her head on his shoulder. "I still love you, James. I'll always love you."

But she shouldn't, he thought. She deserved better than Reed Blackwood. Better than James Dalton. When she snuggled against him, he took her in his arms and wished he could drive a stake through his own traitorous heart.

Today, he would stay with her. And tomorrow, he would ask Zack Ryder to move him as far away from Silver Wolf as possible.

Tandy Stables was closed. The last group of riders was gone and the horses were corralled. James and his WITSEC inspector stood on the wood-framed porch of his mobile home, gazing at the landscape.

As usual, Ryder sucked on a cigarette. "I warned you not to tell her."

James leaned against the porch rail. "Don't start with that 'I told you so' crap. Just get me the hell out of here."

The deputy marshal squinted at the late-day sun. The faint streaks of gray in his sideburns caught the light, and the lines near his eyes turned white against tanned skin. "I can't do that, Dalton."

"You can't or you won't?"

Ryder turned to look at him. "I won't."

Panic strangled James like a noose. "But I can't live here anymore. I can't face Emily every day with a lie crammed between us." He grabbed the beer he'd been nursing and took a hard, gut-clenching swallow. "You have to relocate me."

"I don't *have* to do anything. Was your security breached? Did she threaten to tell anyone about you? Is she gossiping to the neighbors?" The inspector blew a stream of smoke into the air. "No, she isn't. Is she? The woman looks you in the eye and says she still loves you and you're ready to jump ship."

James wanted to take Ryder's cigarette and shove it down his throat. "She looked me in the eye and said I wasn't a killer."

"And you're not."

"Really? You mean I got locked up for nothing?"

The inspector settled lazily into a chair, taking on the casual-cop role he'd been born to play. "You got locked up because a federal judge decided you had to serve time before you were paroled and relocated."

"And here I thought I'd committed a crime."

"Don't be a smart ass."

James glared at the other man. "I was involved in a hit."

Ryder tipped his chair back. "I'm well aware of what you were involved in."

"Of course you are. The great and powerful Oz knows everything."

"And the cowardly lion can't face the woman he loves. Boohoo. Poor baby. He wants to pull a Dorothy and click his heels and go home. Well, guess what? You are home."

The beer went down like poison. "Screw you, Ryder."

"Yeah, screw me. I'm only the guy who agreed to let you break the rules."

And I'm the guy who's dying inside, James thought.

"Tell her the rest of your story, Dalton. Admit the rest of it."

"I can't."

"Yes, you can." Like the chain-smoker he was, Ryder lit another cigarette from the one he'd reduced to a burning stub. "Sit her down and tell her exactly what you did. And if she freaks out, I'll get you the hell out of here. I'll relocate you."

James whipped his head up. "If you don't, I'll split on my own."

"I'll keep my word. But you've got to keep yours. You've got to tell her."

Long after Ryder was gone, James went inside and paced his living room, stalking it from corner to corner. Finally, he grabbed the phone and dialed Emily's number. She picked up on the first ring and he gripped the receiver.

"It's me," he said.

"Oh, thank God. I was getting worried."

"I told you I had to work late."

"I know, but…" Her words drifted, and he cursed the agony he was putting her through. She hadn't slept well last night. She'd tossed and turned in his arms, mumbling in her sleep. Then she'd awakened before him, shadows dogging her eyes.

"Is Corey still at Steven's house?" he asked, knowing the boy spent his summer days there, enjoying the benefit of the home day care program Steven's mother provided.

"Yes, but I'm supposed to pick him up soon."

"Will you ask if they can keep him a little longer?"

"Why? What's wrong?" Her voice practically jumped through the phone. "You sound strange."

He released an anxiety-ridden breath and glanced out the window. "Nothing's wrong. I just need to talk to you."

"Where?"

"Here."

"At the stable? I don't understand why you can't come home."

"I am home. I live at the stable, remember?" And he wanted to give Emily the option of walking away, of deciding if he was worth the trouble.

She arrived a short time later, looking soft and vulnerable in a cotton blouse and an ankle-length skirt. He knew she favored lightweight fabrics, but she kept most of her skin covered, cautious about exposing herself to the sun.

He wanted to take her in his arms and inhale the summer-bound scent of her perfume, but he offered her a seat on the sofa instead. She perched on the edge of it, and he wondered if her pulse was as sketchy as his. She didn't appear to be comfortable. Obviously, she knew something was horribly wrong, even if he'd denied it on the phone.

"Did you ever stop to think of how I was able to testify against the mob?" he asked.

"I assumed you knew damaging things about their

organization," she answered. "Crimes they'd committed."

"I knew details about a murder. A hit I was involved in." Her face went pale but he continued, determined to get the words out. "I spent a year in a federal prison for my part in it. I was an accessory to murder. That's what I was charged with."

Emily's breath rushed out, her emotions splitting in two. This was the man who'd treated her with tenderness and care, who'd helped her battle cancer, who'd taught her rambunctious little brother how to behave like a gentleman? "You told me you were an ex-con, but I thought—"

"That I'd gotten locked up for burglary? I've served time for that, too."

She gripped the side of the couch, praying the room didn't spin. How could he deliberately take someone's life? How could he assist in a murder? "Why, James? Why would you get involved in a hit?"

"Because that's what the West Coast Family told me to do."

"It can't be that simple." She blinked back the tears threatening to fall, and he pushed his hair away from his forehead, exposing the rawboned angles of his face. He looked tough and hard, every bit the ex-con he claimed to be. But he looked like her protector, too. Like the man she'd fallen desperately in love with. "Tell me how it happened."

"It happened because I got in over my head." Catlike, he began to pace, the muscles in his shoulders bunching and rolling. "The West Coast Family isn't an Italian outfit, but they run their operation in a fairly traditional Mafia style. In the beginning, I was building surveillance equipment for one of their lieutenants, and later I became a soldier.''

''A soldier?''

He stopped pacing. ''That's the lowest level of a formal member, but I was still a 'made man.'''

''It sounds like something out of a movie.'' Something she'd seen on a late-night picture show, something a small-town girl from Idaho couldn't relate to.

''Believe it or not, I have a genius IQ.'' His laugh was short and bitter. ''But I'm pretty damn dumb for a smart guy. I never thought I'd be expected to participate in a murder.''

Her stomach clenched, and he turned to look at her. ''Mafia or not, the West Coast Family is a business organization. They're not a bunch of thugs. They have ties to the film industry. The guys at the top own mansions and party with the rich and famous.'' He barked out another laugh. ''What a life.''

Emily pictured him—tall, dark, street-smart James, living in Los Angeles and associating with high-powered criminals. ''You had to know they were dangerous.''

''Sure, I knew. But I'd always thrived on danger, on that quick, don't-get-caught thrill. I was part of the Hollywood mob and I liked it. Being around them gave me a rush.'' He paused, his voice turning hard. ''But the rush ended when they tested my loyalty.''

Emily noticed a muscle ticking in his jaw. An involuntary flinch, she thought. A tense, troubled memory. ''What happened?''

"They called me into the boss's office, and Denny Halloway said he had a job for me."

"Beverly's father?"

"Yes. But I hadn't met Beverly yet. I didn't know Halloway had a daughter. I was familiar with his sons but that's because they were part of his operation." James went on, explaining further. "I figured the job was a burglary of some kind. Everyone knew that alarm systems were one of my specialties. But then Halloway said the job was going down in a few hours, and I realized something was wrong. They wouldn't have brought me in on a robbery in one day."

She waited for him to continue, fearful of what came next, of the details associated with a mob hit, of an act she couldn't begin to imagine.

"The target was a man named Caesar Gibbons, a drug lord who'd cheated Halloway. And since Gibbons was always surrounded by bodyguards, a public hit was planned, using a getaway and a crash car. They knew where Gibbons was having dinner that night, so while he exited his favorite restaurant and entered his limo, a hit man in a getaway car was supposed to shoot him." James shifted his stance, his features taut. "I was brought in to drive the crash car, to 'accidentally' run into anyone who tried to follow the getaway car."

"Why didn't you call the police?" she asked. "Why didn't you warn them a hit was planned?"

"There was no time. I was with Halloway and the triggerman for the rest of the day. And there was a side of me that didn't want to believe it was real, that it was really going to happen."

Her heart pummeled her chest. "But it did."

"Yes, but I botched my part. I couldn't go through with it. Someone in Gibbons's entourage followed the getaway car, but I didn't crash into him. I wanted Halloway's hit man to get caught."

She looked into James's eyes and saw his remorse, the haunting that had been there all along. "Did he get caught?"

"No. I was so damn nervous, I made a quick turn and literally caused an accident anyway. Some old lady barreled right into me and someone else clipped the guy following the triggerman." He frowned at the floor, at a barely visible spot on the carpet. "I stayed at the scene to file an accident report, to act like an innocent bystander who'd gotten caught in the crossfire. At the time, the cops had no idea I was involved, and I didn't tell them. I didn't admit the truth."

She rose, her heartbeat stabilizing. "You admitted it later."

"After the FBI offered to cut me a deal." He lifted his head. "What kind of man does that make me, Emily? What kind of bastard am I?"

She reached for him, but he backed away, refusing to let her touch him, to forgive him for his crime.

Twelve

James knew what was happening. In spite of what he'd done, Emily still loved him. Yet her loyalty, the tenderness he'd craved, only proved how selfish he was.

"Don't pull away from me," she said. "Not now."

"How can you still care about me?"

"Am I supposed to punish you, James? Be your judge and jury? You paid for your sins. You served your time. You testified against the mob."

And he'd asked the Creator for forgiveness, he thought. But somehow, it didn't seem like enough. "Do you have any idea what spending the rest of your life with me will be like?"

Her eyes locked on to his. "I'm willing to find out."

"You shouldn't be. You should stop and think.

Take a good, hard look at who I am.'' Because his legs were as unsteady as his heart, he sat on the edge of a barstool, then reached for the half-empty beer he'd left on the counter. The alcohol was warm, but he took a swig, barely tasting it. ''My life has been full of lies. The last time I saw my sister, the day I said goodbye, I didn't tell her that I would have to serve time. I let her think WITSEC was going to relocate me right away.''

''Why?'' Emily asked. ''So she wouldn't worry about you? What harm is there in that?''

''All I've ever done is lie.'' He discarded the beer, even though his mouth was still dry. ''I never told my wife that I was involved in a hit. She knew I wanted to leave her father's organization, but I didn't have the guts to admit what turned me against them.''

''So you protected her feelings. You—''

''I was protecting *my own* feelings,'' he shot back. ''I was afraid she wouldn't want to be with me if she knew the truth.''

''But it's different between us. You're being honest with me.''

''I almost left. If my WITSEC inspector would have agreed, I'd be gone by now. I'd be in a safe house, waiting to be relocated.''

Stunned, she stepped back. ''How could you do that? How could you even consider it?''

''I was afraid you wouldn't love me anymore. I was afraid I'd lose you anyway.''

''But you didn't.'' She exaggerated her presence with a wide gesture. ''I'm here. I'm right here.''

And looking more vulnerable than ever, he thought.

Loose strands of hair escaped her ponytail and fluttered around her face, like feathers swaying in an emotion-steeped breeze. "Think about it, Emily. Imagine being my wife. Think about what would happen if my security was breached and WITSEC had to move me. You'd have to move, too, to change your name, to become someone new."

When she crossed her arms to hide a small shiver, he realized that she hadn't let her thoughts take her that far.

He went on, driving his point. "You'd never see Diane again. Corey would lose Steven. Hell, you couldn't even visit your parents' graves. Or keep pictures of them. Everything familiar, everything from your childhood would be gone."

She gulped some air into her lungs. "But what if your security isn't breached? We could stay here forever. We could—"

James cut her off. "I'm not worth the risk. You know damn well I'm not."

"That isn't fair." She kept her arms crossed, hugging herself. "You can't expect me to stop loving you. To just let you go."

"Maybe not. But you can't live in a fairy tale, either. Consider what I'm saying. Think about what's right for Corey."

"Why are you doing this?"

"Because my lifestyle could end up hurting you." And dreams were always prettier than reality, he thought. "Up until now, all I wanted was for you to love me, to accept me, to forgive me for the crimes

I committed. But there's more at stake here. There's your future. There's Corey's well-being.''

"You said the mob wouldn't hurt Corey. You said he was safe."

"He is. But how is he going to feel if I end up dead? If some hit man comes along someday and plugs me in the back?''

She shivered again. "Don't say things like that.''

"Why not? You know damn well it could happen.'' He rose, then stopped to study her. "Why didn't you sleep well last night? Why did you toss and turn?''

She glanced out the window, and he followed her gaze to the setting sun, to the red burst of color in the sky. "I was worried.''

"About what?''

"You,'' she admitted.

"Because someone's trying to kill me?''

"Yes.'' She wiped her hands on her skirt and he knew her palms were sweating. "But I only found out about all of this yesterday. Was I supposed to go to bed that night and sleep like a baby?''

"No. Of course not.'' He wished he could hold her, pull her tight against his body and make the rest of the world fade away. But he couldn't. The earth would keep spinning on its axis, and there would always be other people to contend with, other voices to be heard. "We need some time away from each other.''

She couldn't conceal the sudden anger in her eyes. "Why? So you can leave town? Disappear without telling me?''

"I won't leave." He wouldn't become the coward Ryder had accused him of being; he wouldn't run away from the woman he loved. But he wouldn't take advantage of her, either. "If we stay together, I know you'll bring good things to my life, but you can't honestly say the same thing about me."

"Jam—"

He stopped her protest. "Go home, Emily. Visit your friends, chat with your co-workers, look through your photo albums, put some flowers on your parents' graves." He paused for effect. "Then imagine your life without those things."

She flinched, and he knew he'd jarred her emotions. "Am I supposed to imagine putting flowers on your grave, too? Am I supposed to think about that?"

"You already are," he said, as she turned away. "You already are."

Corey traipsed beside Emily with a bouquet of flowers in each hand. He didn't seem to understand why she was so nostalgic this week, but he'd stayed by her side, looking through old photos, laughing at baby pictures of himself. And now they were at the Silver Wolf cemetery where their parents were buried.

Emily hadn't seen James in over seven days, but she thought about him every sleepless night, plagued by the last words they'd spoken. She kept telling herself that she didn't have any doubts, that leaving Silver Wolf didn't frighten her, that she could handle a future with James. But that wasn't true. Knowing that the mob wanted him dead haunted her like a shadow-chasing poltergeist.

Corey looked up at her, and she touched his shoulder. "This is it." She stopped at the marble headstones and wondered what her mom and dad would have thought of James. Her lover. The ex-con. The former mobster.

"Can they see us, Emmy?"

"Who? Our parents?" She knelt on the grass and fought a graveyard chill. What if the mob tortured James? What if they let him bleed to death? "Yes, they can. They're watching us from heaven." Watching their daughter struggle over the man she loved.

Corey set a bouquet of flowers on each grave, then glanced up at the sky. "Is this the only place they can see us from?"

"No. They can see us no matter where we are."

"Even when I'm bad?"

She couldn't help but smile. "You're never bad. Are you?"

"Sometimes I am. On the last day of school, I told Suzy Leery she was stupid, and then Steven and I put some paper towels in the toilets. You're not supposed to do that 'cause it clogs them."

She sat back to study him, not quite sure what to say. His golden hair blew in the breeze and freckles danced across his twitching nose. "Why did you call Suzy Leery stupid?"

He made a pained face. "'Cause she likes me."

"The way girls like boys?"

"Uh-huh. It's stupid."

"Not when you get older. It's nice when you get older." Nice? She reached for a daisy from her mother's bouquet and thought about James, about how much the future frightened her. "The next time you see Suzy, you have to tell her you're sorry."

Corey squirmed like the kid he was. "What about the toilets? Do I gotta tell them I'm sorry, too?"

She shook her head, and suddenly they both burst out laughing. And at that silly, childlike moment, she knew her parents were laughing, too.

"Are you ready to go?" she asked, after a few minutes of silence.

He nodded and got to his feet. As they cut across the lawn, he glanced at the flower in her hand. "What are you gonna do with that?"

She adjusted the daisy. "Give it to Lily Mae."

"The lady James works for?"

"That's right."

"Are you gonna see James, too?"

"No, not today." She knew he would keep his distance. "Lily Mae and I are going on a picnic."

"Be careful in the sun, Emmy."

Touched by his concern, she ruffled his hair. "I'm wearing my lotion. And I have a hat in the car, too. Besides, we're going to try to stay in the shade."

"Me and Steven are helping his mom bake cookies today. She thinks you and James should get married. I think so, too. And so does Steven. We want to wear those bow-tie suits and eat cake and stuff."

Her heart pole-vaulted to her throat. "Is that the only reason you think James and I should get married?"

"No." He reached for a fallen leaf on the ground and kept walking. "I'd like to have him as my dad. Or my brother. Or—" Puzzled, he stalled. "What would he be if you married him?"

My husband, she thought. My lifelong partner. The man the West Coast Family wanted to kill. Dear God, she thought. How could she stay with him? How could she subject herself to that kind of pain?

Emily ignored Corey's question and dropped him off for his cookie-baking activity. Gripping the steering wheel, she proceeded to Lily Mae's house. The older lady lived in a ranch-style home surrounded by foliage and timbered mountains.

Lily Mae met her at the door with a container of fresh-squeezed lemonade. Emily handed her the flower. The other woman snapped the stem and tucked the daisy behind her ear.

"Ready to go?" Emily asked.

"You bet."

They didn't need to travel far to find a comfortable spot on Lily Mae's property. Emily unpacked the picnic basket and Lily Mae settled onto their blanket with a comfy wiggle.

"This makes me feel young again," she said.

"It's peaceful here." Emily gazed at the trees that weaved their way into a forest. "I miss being outdoors."

"You look cute in that hat." Lily Mae poured the lemonade. "Straw suits you."

Emily curbed a giggle. Lily Mae had an odd way about her, but her unusual approach to life was honest and refreshing. After filling two paper plates with fried chicken, diced fruit and potato salad, she offered one to Lily Mae.

The other woman accepted it greedily. "Aren't you going to ask about him?"

Emily reached for her fork. "Who?"

"James."

Her stomach tensed. She'd spent the past week imagining him at the stables, working in the sun, his skin glowing from hard-earned sweat. Her James, she thought. Her shape-shifter. The man who might live; the man who might die. "How is he?"

"Keeping busy. But he's brooding a lot. I guess you two are having a little trouble."

She couldn't tell Lily Mae what was wrong, just as she hadn't been able to tell Diane. But this was what James had warned her about. Being in a relationship with him meant keeping secrets. "I was hoping we could talk about Harvey."

"Harvey?" Lily Mae started. "Now why would you want to talk about that old codger?"

"You danced with him at my party."

"One silly dance. It didn't mean a thing."

"Didn't it?" Emily picked at her food. "I heard you two went for a walk that night."

"It was just a short walk."

"James thinks you and Harvey were lovers once."

"Does he?" Lily Mae blinked, then sighed, unable to mask her emotions. "And here I thought no one knew."

"I don't think anyone does. James figured it out on his own."

The older woman turned to look at the forest, scrutinizing the trees that bled into the mountains. "I came from money, and Harvey's family was dirt-poor. He used to smile at me in town, and my heart would pitter-patter. Just like rain falling on a roof."

Emily nodded. She knew the feeling well.

Lily Mae went on. "My parents were rather snobbish for country folks, and they had a prestigious suitor in mind for me, a young man they wanted me to marry."

"Did you agree to marry him?"

"Yes. I wasn't strong enough to defy my parents, particularly my mother. She was a demanding woman." Lily Mae turned away from the trees. "A month before the wedding, I drove to the river. It was late, after midnight, and I wanted to be alone. But Harvey happened to be there."

Emily tried to picture the older couple when they were young, but all she could see was James and herself. "Did you make love with him that night?"

"Yes. And we saw each other after that, too. We continued to meet at the river. But we didn't dare let anyone know."

"What happened?"

"I couldn't face my parents with the truth, so I married the man they'd chosen for me. Harvey was devastated." Lily Mae frowned at her plate. "Harvey enlisted in the army, and when his tour ended, he came back to Silver Wolf, then landed a job with the post office. I got divorced and married someone else. I've been married three times."

"But never to Harvey," Emily put in.

"No. Never to him. By the time my third marriage ended, I was through with men."

"And now?"

Lily Mae blushed like a schoolgirl. "And now I'm

sneaking around with Harvey. Can you imagine? Two old fools kissing in the moonlight?''

Emily's heart clenched. ''I think it's romantic.''

''Do you?'' The gray-haired woman ducked her head. ''We feel silly to let people know we're dating.''

''You shouldn't. You've earned your right to be happy. And so has Harvey.'' Emily knew the retired postal worker had never married. ''Do you regret all those years you spent apart?''

''Yes, I do. More than I can say. There's nothing worse than missing the man you love.'' Her voice turned sad. ''Nothing at all.''

Emily appeared like a watery image in the distance, an enchanted creature in denim, cotton and lace. James stood in the breezeway of the barn, reminding himself to breathe. As she approached, she removed her hat and fluffed her hair. The honey-blond strands settled around her face, and his fingers itched to touch. But he remained still, keeping his hands at his sides.

A horse nickered behind him, but he ignored the friendly sound. His heart was pounding like a pow-wow drum and his pulse spun like a fringed and feathered dancer whirling to the beat.

He wanted to kiss her, to thrust his tongue into her mouth, to drop to his knees and peel off her jeans, to make her head fall back and her body convulse. But the sexual urges only made him more nervous than he already was, and he cursed his raging libido.

He missed her. God help him, he did.

She stopped in front of him, and they gazed at each other. When her breath hitched, James knew he had to accept whatever the Creator had in store for him. Happiness, heartbreak. Whatever it was, he couldn't change the outcome.

"You're worth the risk," she said.

Everything, including his pounding heart, went still. Soundless. Motionless. He couldn't hear the horses anymore. The wind stopped rustling through trees, the heady scents from the barn disappeared.

"How can you be sure?" he asked.

"Because I did all the things you told me to do. I evaluated every aspect of my life."

His legs nearly shook. "What about Corey?"

"My brother loves you."

He had to be sure. He had to make certain she'd thought this through. "What if there's a security breach and I have to relocate someday? This is your home. You grew up in Silver Wolf. You and Corey have ties here."

She moved closer, just a little closer. "Home is where the heart is, James. There's a reason someone came up with that saying."

"It wasn't someone being hunted by the mob. It wasn't someone in our situation."

"Does it matter who came up with it? Or why?"

He couldn't bear the thought of taking anything away from her. "What about your memories? The pictures of your parents?"

She glanced up, as though searching for heaven, for her family. "I'll always have my memories, no matter where I live. And I'll remember my parents, with or without pictures.''

He pressed the issue, pushing her further. ''What if someone kills me? What if the mob—''

''Don't.'' She cut him off. ''Don't talk about that.''

''We can't ignore it,'' he argued. ''We can't pretend it isn't real, that the possibility doesn't exist.''

''I know.'' She fidgeted with her hat, still holding it, keeping her restless hands busy. ''But we can't dwell on death, either.''

''You're afraid.'' He could see the fear in her eyes, the sheen of tears just below the surface.

''Of course I'm afraid. And somewhere deep down, I'll always be afraid. But I *have* to believe WITSEC will protect you. That they'll keep you safe. Lily Mae told me there's nothing worse than missing the man you love. And she's right. I've missed you so badly this week, I could hardly stand it.'' Her voice quavered, trembling softly. ''I want you to be part of my life, no matter what happens.''

''Oh, God.'' James stepped forward, and they embraced, their emotions tangling like vines. He inhaled her perfume, the airy fragrance misting her skin. He longed to have her, to keep her as close as possible. But he battled a fist of guilt, too. ''I'm ashamed of my past.''

''I know, but it's over now.''

''I wronged society.''

Emily needed to free her hands, so she dropped her hat and let it float to the barn floor. ''I trust you. I'll always trust you.'' Unable to help herself, she traced his features, skimming the arch of his brows, the slant of his cheekbones, the determined angle of his jaw. What would she do without him? How would she survive?

"You deserve better," he said. "Better than an ex-con."

"Don't apologize." He wasn't the fairy-tale prince from her adolescent dreams, but he was her protector, the flesh and blood man God had brought to her door. "Do you still love me, James?"

He released a labored breath. "You know I do."

"Then show me."

That was all it took. He clutched her hand and led her to his house. But not to the bedroom. She found herself in the bathroom, being stripped of her clothes. Her blood flowed hot and anxious through her veins. He undressed himself, and she watched, waiting, wondering what came next. They'd never showered together, never caressed beneath a sultry spray of water.

In the silence, she studied him—the tall, powerful form of his body—those wide, sturdy shoulders, the flat, hard plane of his stomach, his fingers on his fly, unzipping his jeans. When his chest rose and fell, she knew he was as anxious as she was.

Naked, they climbed into the tub and turned on the shower. But there was no time to bathe, to gather the soap, to lather each other's skin.

James dropped right to his knees.

He licked her as desperately as he could, shocking her with hot, blinding pleasure. Emily bucked on contact, and she knew this was more than foreplay. This was James, taking what he needed, branding her in his mind.

Like a ship on a turbulent sea, she rocked against the motion, against the wetness, against the water raining over his face. His tongue delved deep, teasing her, flicking in and out, moving in a sweet, searing rhythm.

Steam rose in the air, as damp and dewy as her skin. A throaty moan escaped her lips, and he held her against his mouth, urging her release, the blast of desire that slammed into her system, then left her molten and weak.

But before she could draw her next breath, he rose to kiss her, to nudge her against the shower wall, to battle the condom he'd left on the side of the tub.

Emily blinked through the haze, through the force of being in love. His body glistened, rock hard and erect. She reached for him, and for a moment, for one slow, dizzying moment, he simply held her.

Then he plunged swift and deep. She could feel her muscles clamp around him, keeping him tight and secure. Her heart pounded with every thrust, with every power-driven jolt. She moved with him, stroke for stroke, soul to soul. The hunger to mate fevered her blood, and she saw the same craving, the same want, in his eyes.

And then he climaxed inside her, stealing her breath, banishing her thoughts, making everything but the sweet, slick sensation of making love disappear.

Afterward, he pressed his forehead to hers, and she ran her hands up and down his back. The shower was still running, spraying them like a waterfall.

''Marry me,'' he said against her lips.

She kissed him in response, a long, lingering kiss. His body remained joined with hers, making his proposal warm and erotic.

''When?'' she asked.

''Now.''

''Right now?'' She rocked her hips, and he smiled.

''Maybe not right now. But soon. As soon as we can manage it.'' He drew her closer, filling her body, steeping her heart, making a promise she knew he would keep.

Epilogue

On the most important day of his life, James stood next to Zack Ryder. Dressed in black tuxedos, they waited outside a quaint little hilltop chapel that presided over Silver Wolf with a rein of beauty. The terrain was dotted with flowers, and the sun had begun to set, painting the summer sky with strokes of gold, crimson and blue.

Ryder stepped back to study him. "You look good, Dalton."

James shook his head. He'd actually asked a deputy marshal to be his best man. A lawman. A federal cop. "You look okay, too."

"Okay?" Ryder adjusted his tie. "I look handsome as hell."

James smiled. "For an old man."

The WITSEC inspector made a tough-guy face, but

his eyes sparkled nonetheless. "I could kick your young, cocky ass any day."

"Any day but today." James's mood turned serious. "I don't want to fight today."

Ryder nodded, slipping into the same earnest frame of mind. For a short while they remained silent, watching a squirrel skitter up a nearby tree. Finally, the WITSEC inspector spoke. "I've got some news about your family."

James's heart skipped a beat. "My sister?"

"It's good news. She married her lover about a year ago, and they're expecting their second child."

An intense feeling came over him. He took a deep breath and pictured Heather back in Texas, married and pregnant, with his son by her side. "What about their first child? Justin," he added, picturing the baby boy he'd given away.

"I heard that little tyke is growing like a weed." Ryder reached for a cigarette, then reconsidered, leaving the pack in his pocket. "They're a happy family."

James blinked back the moisture that came to his eyes. "Will you let them know I'm happy, too? Get word to them somehow?"

"Are you sure you don't want me to arrange a phone call for you? Are you sure you don't want to talk to your sister yourself?"

"I think it would be easier if you did it." Because talking to Heather about Justin would only make him miss the boy even more.

"Then I'll take care of it," the deputy said.

"Thank you." James gazed at the town below, at the simple rooftops and quiet country roads. "I'm going to be all right, Ryder. I'm done screwing up my life.''

''You bet you are. And WITSEC is going to make damn sure you remain safe.'' The older man checked his watch. ''We better go inside. It's about that time.''

The chapel was filled with friends who'd come to share this special day, to witness James and Emily take a vow. James saw Lily Mae and Harvey in the first pew, both decked out in their Sunday finest. Corey, the tuxedoed ring bearer, waited at the entrance with a pretty little flower girl Emily had chosen. Diane served as the matron of honor, and her husband had lent himself out as an usher. Steven wasn't in the ceremony, but he wore a tux just like Corey's, proud of his silk lapels and boutonniere.

The procession began and, one by one, the wedding party made their way down the aisle. When the bride finally appeared, James couldn't keep his eyes off her. A traditional white gown draped her slim form, and a veil, as sheer as a whisper, covered her face.

She moved with grace and elegance, and he watched with awe and wonder. After she lifted her veil, their gazes locked and held. At that life-altering moment, the Cherokee incantation swirled between them, and he knew she had come to draw away his soul.

It wasn't time to kiss her, but it didn't matter. He leaned into her and she brushed his mouth, sending a ripple of warmth through his body. The sweet scent of her bouquet filled his nostrils, and he thanked the Creator for the woman who'd given him hope, who loved and trusted him.

Together, they turned to the minister, ready to repeat their vows, to face the world and conquer their fears, to share their dreams and become husband and wife.

* * * * *

*Watch for Sheri WhiteFeather's next
Silhouette Desire,
A KEPT WOMAN,
in which Zack Ryder gets his
own story, coming in April.*

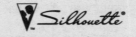

Silhouette Desire

DIXIE BROWNING

tantalizes readers with her latest romance from Silhouette Desire:

Driven to Distraction
(Silhouette Desire #1568)

You'll feel the heat when a beautiful columnist finds herself compelled by desire for a long-legged lawman. Can close proximity bring out their secret longings?

Available March 2004 at your favorite retail outlet.

If you enjoyed what you just read,
then we've got an offer you can't resist!

Take 2 bestselling
love stories FREE!
Plus get a FREE surprise gift!

Clip this page and mail it to Silhouette Reader Service™

IN U.S.A.
3010 Walden Ave.
P.O. Box 1867
Buffalo, N.Y. 14240-1867

IN CANADA
P.O. Box 609
Fort Erie, Ontario
L2A 5X3

YES! Please send me 2 free Silhouette Desire® novels and my free surprise gift. After receiving them, if I don't wish to receive anymore, I can return the shipping statement marked cancel. If I don't cancel, I will receive 6 brand-new novels every month, before they're available in stores! In the U.S.A., bill me at the bargain price of $3.57 plus 25¢ shipping and handling per book and applicable sales tax, if any*. In Canada, bill me at the bargain price of $4.24 plus 25¢ shipping and handling per book and applicable taxes**. That's the complete price and a savings of at least 10% off the cover prices—what a great deal! I understand that accepting the 2 free books and gift places me under no obligation ever to buy any books. I can always return a shipment and cancel at any time. Even if I never buy another book from Silhouette, the 2 free books and gift are mine to keep forever.

225 SDN DNUP
326 SDN DNUQ

Name	(PLEASE PRINT)	
Address	Apt.#	
City	State/Prov.	Zip/Postal Code

* Terms and prices subject to change without notice. Sales tax applicable in N.Y.
** Canadian residents will be charged applicable provincial taxes and GST.
All orders subject to approval. Offer limited to one per household and not valid to current Silhouette Desire® subscribers.
® are registered trademarks of Harlequin Books S.A., used under license.

Silhouette® Desire®

The captivating family saga of the Danforths continues with

Sin City Wedding
by
KATHERINE GARBERA
(Silhouette Desire #1567)

When ex-flame Larissa Nelson showed up on Jacob Danforth's doorstep with a child she claimed was his, the duty-bound billionaire demanded they marry. A quickie wedding in Vegas joined Jacob and the shy librarian in a marriage of convenience…but living as husband and wife stirred passions that neither could deny—nor resist.

DYNASTIES: THE DANFORTHS

**A family of prominence…
tested by scandal, sustained by passion!**

Available March 2004 at your favorite retail outlet.

Silhouette Desire®

COMING NEXT MONTH

#1567 SIN CITY WEDDING—Katherine Garbera
Dynasties: The Danforths
When ex-flame Larissa Nelson showed up on Jacob Danforth's doorstep with a child she claimed was his, the duty-bound billionaire demanded they marry. A quickie wedding in Vegas joined Jacob and the shy librarian in a marriage of convenience, but living as husband and wife stirred passions that neither could deny…nor resist.

#1568 DRIVEN TO DISTRACTION—Dixie Browning
An unofficial investigation led both Maggie Riley and Ben Hunter to sign up for a painting class. As artists, the advice columnist and ex-cop were complete failures, but as lovers they were *red-hot*. Soon the mystery they'd come to solve was taking a back seat to their unquenchable desires!

#1569 PRETENDING WITH THE PLAYBOY—Cathleen Galitz
Texas Cattleman's Club: The Stolen Baby
Outwardly charming, secretly cynical, Alexander Kent held no illusions about love. Then the former FBI agent was paired with prim and innocent Stephanie Firth on an undercover mission. Posing as a couple led to some heated moments. Too bad intense lovemaking wasn't enough to base forever on. Or was it?

#1570 PRIVATE INDISCRETIONS—Susan Crosby
Behind Closed Doors
Former bad boy Sam Remington returned to his hometown after fifteen years with only one thing in mind: Dana Sterling. The former golden girl and U.S. Senator had been the stuff of fantasies for adolescent Sam…and still was. But when threats put Dana in danger, could Sam put his desires aside and save her?

#1571 A TEMPTING ENGAGEMENT—Bronwyn Jameson
He'd woken with a hangover—and a very naked nanny in his bed. Trouble was, single dad Mitch Goodwin couldn't remember what had happened the night before. And when Emily Warner left without a word, he *had* to lure her back. For his son's sake, of course. But keeping his hands off the innocently seductive Emily was harder than he imagined….

#1572 LIKE A HURRICANE—Roxanne St. Claire
Developer Quinn McGrath could always recognize a hot property. And sassy Nicole Whitaker was definitely that. Discovering that Nicole was blockading his business deal didn't faze him. They were adversaries in business—but it was pleasuring the voluptuous beauty that Quinn couldn't stop thinking about.

SDCNM0204